Molly Jo Daisy

Being the New Kid

Mary Louise Morris

Illustrations: Mary Louise Morris

My heartfelt thanks **to my guest artists:**
Ashlyn Lindow, Henry Morris, and Millie Morris

Each of them contributed artwork for the story.

~~~

"Home is a feeling, Molly Jo. Home is right here, right now, wherever we are. Let's feel it in our hearts."

Mary Sparkle Silver Press
A branch of Morris Smith LLC

Copyright © 2020 by Mary Louise Morris

Maple River, Maine, is a fictitious town written from the author's imagination.

Printed in the United States of America
First Printing, 2020

ISBN 978-1-7352512-0-2 (paperback)
ISBN 978-1-7352512-1-9 (ebook)

Library of Congress Control Number: 2020912086

Visit us at www.facebook.com/MollyJoDaisy

CONTENTS

DEDICATION

Thank you to my husband, Dave, and my entire family,
who have encouraged me greatly to write Molly Jo
stories. I love and appreciate you.

Thank you to all the "new kids" in the world. Whether
you've moved across town, across the country, or simply
changed schools - you know what it's like to
start all over again in a new place.

A special thanks to three of Molly Jo's biggest fans:
Millie Morris, Henry Morris, and Ashlyn Lindow

Thank you to my friend, Linda, who has an
adorable giraffe that inspired Rudy,
an endearing character you will meet.

Thank you to my Maine friend, Jane,
who told me about a sweet New England treat
that I included in the story.

Molly Jo's story shows you how you can
turn things around in your head
from heartsick to hopeful,
from nervous to brave
and from worry to wonder.

Always look beyond the rough spots
and plant your heart there.

PREFACE

Would you like to move to a new place and start over making friends? Would you like to be a new kid at school? If you do, raise your hand. If you're not raising your hand, that's alright, too.

Ten-year-old Molly Jo Daisy isn't raising her hand. She may be like you! She was perfectly happy in her Nashville home, living across the street from her best friend. But her Dad got a new job, and their family is moving 1,201 miles away to Maple River, Maine, with no plans to return to the place that Molly Jo calls "her perfect home."

But wait a minute, before you decide you would never in a million years move. Like Molly Jo, you may discover that moving can be one of the best things to ever happen to you. Of course, anytime you do something big in your life, there will be challenges. But there will also be fun, new experiences you never knew possible.

That's why Molly Jo, after she gets over the initial adjustment of moving, decides she is "never looking back with a sad heart." She realizes, despite the awkward moments of being new in Maple River, marvelous things are unfolding in her life. She wouldn't trade them for anything.

If you and your family are planning to move, just know that I have moved 19 times in my life, and I understand your concerns.

When I was a kid, my parents told me that they hoped to build a brand-new home a few blocks from where we lived. I wished I could tell you I was a brave kid and that I cheered my parents on, but I didn't. In fact, I secretly hoped they would never bring up the topic again. That was not very brave of me to be reluctant to move just a few blocks away.

I moved three times as a kid, but it was when I was quite young. But when I married my high school sweetheart, we began moving every two or three years. My husband was in the Air Force for 20 years, so he and I moved frequently and far along with our two sons.

Our sons, Dan and Tom, learned firsthand what it was like to be the "new kids" at school, and they did it enthusiastically, but not without the ups and downs of leaving friends and making new friends. I admire and appreciate their attitudes because we moved often with the Air Force. Through it all, they became very adaptable people with life experiences that people only dream about. And the tradition continues with their own families.

Please don't agonize about moving because things will look up. I totally understand why it can seem strange at first, but give it some time, and you will feel at home again. Maybe you will like your new home even better. That happened to me!

Molly Jo isn't quite a "trooper" as the story begins, but she soon discovers pleasant surprises in her new hometown. With the help of her Grandma and the push of her younger, exuberant brother, won't you come with me to see how Molly Jo works out her concerns?

If you know of new kids at your school or in your neighborhood, you can help them more than you realize.

Try these ways to welcome new kids, or come up with your own ideas:

❀ Be their lunch pal.

❀ Show them around your school and neighborhood.

❀ Introduce them to your friends.

❀ Invite them to play.

❀ Take cookies or homemade pie to their family.

By welcoming them, you will help them feel at home more quickly.

Thank you for doing your share to make new kids feel welcome and appreciated.

If you are a new kid yourself, I hope someone welcomes you with a kind heart.

But don't wait for someone to be your friend. Someone out there is needing a friend, and that person could be you.

With love,

Mary Louise Morris

Molly Jo Daisy Being the New Kid

CHAPTER 1:
A LONG WAYS FROM HOME

For 100% sure, some things in life are just plain hard. At least for me. My family is moving far from anywhere I have known. Never in a million years did I expect we would move to Maine. Maple River, Maine, to be exact.

I loved living in Nashville on Chesterfield Lane, across the street from my best friend Melissa, but my Dad's job changed. He is going to be working with my Uncle Jim at his woodshop in Maine.

The end of summer is here, and our road trip from Nashville to Maple River is 1,201 miles. That is further than I've ever been in my whole life. I want to shout to the entire world, "My family is moving!" and maybe someone will pull us back to Tennessee where we belong. My life is feeling like a tangled mess.

At this very moment, the only home we have is inside our van. Our house on Chesterfield Lane already belongs to another family. Our new house in Maple River is sitting empty, waiting for us to arrive.

Mom explains, "Molly Jo, you're silly to think our home is inside this van, but you are right because we are between here and there. Let's have fun wherever we are and call it home because we're all together."

My little sister Grace laughed. She says living in our van is fun. My brother John, who is almost always right, says, "Technically, our home is at our hotel room."

He's right. At night we sleep at hotels.

My Grandma put both hands over her heart and said, "Home is a feeling, Molly Jo. Home is right here, right now, wherever we are. Let's feel it in our hearts."

1,201 miles is exceptionally far to go in a van with Grace, John, my Mom, my Dad, and Grandma. Our van is packed in every nook and cranny, and I can't wait till we get there and unpack all this craziness.

The crate on the roof of our van holds Dad's woodworking tools and my glass piggy bank and Grandma's jewelry. Dad said we should bring all our fragile possessions with us, so they don't get lost or broken on the moving truck.

On our three-day road trip to Maine, I stuffed myself with hamburger sliders, peanut butter crackers, and a bag of popcorn that stained my fingers yellow. My Mom usually never lets us eat junk food, although I love every tasty bite. Nothing about moving to Maine is normal.

We kids are staying busy on our road trip while Mom and Dad follow the map to Maple River. John keeps begging me to play car bingo with him, but I prefer doodling in my new blue journal and doing puzzle books. I cross my heart that I will be a nicer sister when we get to Maple River. I promise I will.

Grandma told me not to work puzzles in the van because it makes me dizzy, and she's right. My stomach churns like it's upside down and inside out. I don't know why I don't listen to her because this happens whenever we take a road trip.

Grace gets restless in the van, so Grandma lets her play with her small red radio. Grace is supposed to keep the volume on level three, not a bit higher, or Grandma says she will take the batteries out of it and put it away. I wonder if she really would. Grace is happiest when her teddy bear Smokey sits on her lap.

We all have our places in the van. Mom and Dad sit up front. Grandma sits behind the driver's seat in the middle row with Grace. John and I share the back seat. Grandma oversees the controls for the air conditioning, and she likes to keep it cold in the van, so I keep my fleece blanket on my lap.

Grandma has a black screen that sticks to her window to keep out the sun. Most of the time, she reads bird magazines and watercolor books with a giant magnifying glass that hangs from a string around her neck and rests on her chest. I might be bad for noticing, but she moves her lips when she reads the words even though she is not reading them aloud.

Sometimes she plays car bingo with John and tells super funny bug stories to Grace and Smokey, using her high-pitched little-kid voice. I pretend I'm not listening to her stories anymore, but I still love them even though I'm ten.

The thing I love about Grandma is that she comes prepared for everything! She packed her tall red traveling bag with games and playing cards and foldable binoculars. And she has pencils and paper and scissors and spicy mints, and cherry cough drops, and bandages, and a pink package of tissues. Oh, and a book with license plate labels from every state.

Every time we see a license plate from a new state, we place the sticker in the book. If we fill up the book, then we saw cars from every single state. Currently, we have 16.

Grandma gave spending money to each of us kids for our trip to use any way we wanted. We shop in the gas station stores because they have fun stuff we don't see in regular stores – like postcards and souvenirs and vending machines where you can get rings and treasures.

I got a plastic egg with a tiny magnifying glass inside that I can use when I read small words. Grandma told John and me that we can make our own magnifying glass by cutting a circle from the rounded side of a plastic bottle and then putting a few drops of water on it. If you look through the water drops, things look larger. I wish I could try it right here, right now, but I guess not while we are in our van.

John brought his rock collection with him. Well, not all of it, just his favorite rocks, the ones that sparkle and glimmer and the extra rare ones. He carries them in a cigar box that Grandma gave to him that used to belong to Grandpa Daisy.

Yesterday John parked his cigar box underneath his seat in the van. When Dad slammed on the brakes to avoid hitting a duck on the road, the cigar box slid to the position ahead, and his rocks flew all over the place. I mean everywhere, and I saw Dad's face in the rear-view mirror, and he had that "what's-going-on-back-there" expression.

When the rocks were scattering all over the floor, there was silence in the van. Dead silence. Nobody said anything. Nothing. Nada. Not a word.

John kept his head down, and Dad kept driving. Mom cupped her hands on each side of her face and looked down at the rocks on the floor. Grace blurted out, "I see one here. I see one there."

Grandma patched the awkwardness by saying, "Who is going to help John put his rocks back in the box?" So, we all started picking up the ones we could find. Dad says, "Let's wait until we pull over to find the rest of them," but he asked Mom to check around the gas pedal and brake for them.

Mom unbuckled for just a moment and got on her hands and knees to check the floor around Dad's feet. She found two of John's rocks there. Whew! John didn't say a single word except "Oops."

I noticed Grandma was fiddling with something, so I peeked around the seat. She was pulling everything out of her purse, filling up her lap with chewing gum packets, sunglasses, a hairbrush, a bag of quarters, and a red notebook. Finally, she found two rubber bands for John to keep his cigar box closed.

John knows more about rocks and bugs than anyone I know. He even memorized their scientific names – like schist and quartzite – and that's smart for a 3rd grader. John knows the technical reason why some rocks change colors when they get wet.

On this road trip, we stayed in two double-story hotels and went swimming every single day. Grace gets excited to fill the ice buckets in our hotel room. One of the super-duper things about sleeping in the hotel is that John and I get to sleep on cots. Our room doesn't have enough beds for everyone in our family, but who cares? I wish I could always sleep on a cot.

Mom and Dad started a new tradition on our trip. They collect Christmas ornaments from places we visit. My favorite one so far is a sparkly gold ornament that looks like a lemon slice. It says, "West Virginia" on it. I love how it dazzles in the light.

To our surprise, Mom and Dad allow us kids to do things on our trip that they would never usually allow. Please don't tell anyone, but I didn't change my socks or underwear from yesterday. I guess when a family moves, parents have new things to worry about, and kids' smelly undies aren't one of them.

And another thing I still cannot believe is that Mom and Dad let me eat cinnamon rolls three days in a row, my absolute favorite thing in the world. The hotel has scrambled eggs, but they are watery, and might I say yucky and chewy? Nothing like the fluffy, cheesy eggs Dad makes for us at home.

We have a scientific reason for not eating nutritious snacks on our trip. The cooler that Grandma packed with healthy treats – grapes, apples, string cheese, bananas, carrots, and meat sandwiches – went missing from our van.

Dad accidentally left it behind at the first gas station where we stopped. While the gas was pumping into our van, Dad repacked our luggage and boxes so that things wouldn't slide around in the back. He must have taken the cooler out and forgotten to put it back in. We didn't know that it was missing until we stopped at a state park for our first picnic lunch. That was a downer for sure.

I remember. We bustled out of the car and raced to the picnic table under a shade tree. Mom and Dad lingered behind to gather the picnic things. Something was very wrong when Grandma turned around half-way and said, "Come on, kids. We all need to head back to the van to see if Mom and Dad need help with the lunch stuff."

When we reached the van, we heard the terrible news that the cooler with our favorite snacks and lunches was a goner. Goodbye, string cheese, lemonade, and bananas. After using the restroom and guzzling a long sip of cold water from the fountain, we all scrambled back into the van.

Dad gazed at Mom with his puppy dog eyes and said, "We just have to laugh about our missing cooler!" Mom shook her head and told him, "It is not funny. Not funny at all." She wasn't laughing either. Grandma said, "All those sandwiches I packed! What a shame, but it's not worth turning around to get it. Maybe when we get to the next town, we can get a new cooler."

So, we drove down the road until we found a diner, which Dad says is the best kind of restaurant. We ordered chocolate malts and chili dogs, which turned out to be the best meal of the whole trip, in my opinion, of course.

Mom said we had to order something green too. So, I got broccoli, and John got peas – my first worst. Grace ordered asparagus sticks, her favorite. Grandma ordered homemade vegetable soup and crackers, and you would think she had won a hundred dollars. She said it was that delicious.

My Mom has a clipboard with lists of things she wants to get done. When she finishes something on the list, she makes a big red checkmark next to it. She has a checklist for getting us kids registered at school, a list of all our moving boxes, what's inside them, and a list of people that need to know our new address.

Dad says everything will get done in due time, and not to stress about it now. All I know is that Mom hasn't been humming lately like she usually does. But she finally agreed with Dad and said she would put her clipboard away for a few days. Ever since then, our real Mom is back – which washes away some of my worries.

Grandma says things will return to normal when we are settled, and she will make cheesy potatoes the first night in our new house. And she promised she'd help make our home wonderfully comfortable. If anybody can make things cozy, Grandma can. Even though we'll be in a strange house in a town in Maine where I've never been, Grandma will help more than anything.

The plan was for our family to move to Maine last June, so we would have all summer to settle before school. But that didn't happen because we had to wait for our house to sell in Nashville. And that took all summer long.

Instead of moving in June, we did what Dad calls "Plan B," which means stay all summer in Nashville and hang out with my best friend Melissa, who knows me even better than I know myself. I would never complain about Plan B unless there was a Plan C to not move at all. That would have been my pick, but I don't think anybody cared what I thought.

As we crossed the state line from New Hampshire into Maine, there was a big welcome sign, much like the other states we passed.

The sign said: "Welcome to Maine. The Way Life Should Be."

It almost seemed like the sign was there for our family because we were all cheering when we saw it. I cheered because I can't wait to get out of the van, but I think Grandma and John cheered because they love this kind of crazy adventure. All of us, even me, are in awe of how close we are to the ocean. Now I know why Dad said we can go to the beach in the summer!

We still had to drive another hour or so to get to Maple River, but when we arrived, it took my breath away just a bit. The downtown sidewalks are made of red bricks, and there are giant pots of colorful flowers on every corner. But the neatest thing is the gold sign that hangs above the street that says, "Welcome to Maple River, Maine. We live a charmed life."

I asked Grandma what that means, and she said, "Well, Molly Jo, I think it means that this is a town of satisfied people. We must be moving to a mighty fine place!"

The town looks kind enough, more adorable than I expected, but it's not home. It's not home at all. Being here feels like we are on the other side of the world. How come we had to be the ones to move?

I cried a puddle of tears when we pulled out of our driveway in Nashville, and now, now that our road trip is over, my worst thoughts are coming true. My head is missing everything and everyone I left behind.

Grandma likes to say, "We will have *fun no matter what.*" I wonder if she is just saying that or if she really believes it in her heart.

Moving far away feels scary and hard. Grandma keeps telling me I can change my thoughts, and everything will start looking up for me. I don't understand how that can possibly be true, but Grandma says it's like cough medicine. Cough medicine works even though we don't know how. It just does. I suppose not everything is explainable.

So maybe she is right. Changing my thinking might make a difference. But if it were that easy, why wouldn't everyone change their thoughts?

CHAPTER 2:
OUR NEW HOUSE IN MAPLE RIVER

So our new house is just a few blocks from downtown Maple River. I don't know why, but I think I was holding my breath when Dad turned the van onto our new street. I wondered which house is ours, as I looked up and down on both sides. Mom says it's the third house on the left. Seems so weird – it's exciting and scary all at the same time. I got goosebumps as we got close.

When we pulled into the driveway, my eyes were about to roll off my face and drop onto the ground. Our new house looks like a twin to our place in Nashville. I am not kidding.

In fact, I almost thought Dad moved our old house from Tennessee to Maine. I imagined him driving a truck with our old house on it, but that would be ridiculous. Yet, both houses have two stories with a big front porch and giant trees in the yard. They look so much the same!

Between you and me, without a single itty-bitty doubt, I know it's not the same house, but at first, I wasn't entirely sure, and no way will I tell John that. Or anyone else. Ever. I am convinced John would have never thought it was the same house.

I love that our new house has a porch like our old house. My parents say that a house is not a home if it doesn't have a porch. And they are serious about that. And Grandma too. She likes to watch birds from the porch, and sometimes she just sits on the porch swing and does nothing, which is when I love talking to her about things.

As we all got out of our van and stepped into the front yard and onto our porch for the first time, I noticed something fantastic! Our new house has a sparkly blue and green stained-glass window right above the front door. Everyone who visits us is going to think we are fancy people.

And our mailbox is right on our porch. Why isn't everybody's mailbox on the porch? I can get the mail in my pajamas. Is that crazy or what?

When we stepped inside our new house for the first time, I knew for 100% positivity that this was a different house. The floors are wooden and creaky, the windows are tall, the kitchen has two ovens (which put a big smile on my Mom's face), and the stairs don't have carpeting. As we walked around, I could see wallpaper in almost every room, and I love it. Hearts and pineapples and dots and checks.

Dad proclaimed, "This wallpaper is old fashioned and hideous and will be the first thing to be ripped down."
Hideous? I love it. We never had wallpaper before.
Mom replied, "I'll oversee the wallpaper project."

Maybe we'll get to keep it. I hope! Grandma seemed to have no opinion about it, but sometimes she just doesn't say anything. She says sometimes it is better to keep quiet than to say anything at all.

This house has a funny, musty smell and I wanted to open all the windows for fresh air. Grandma says it will disappear when we clean and fill the house up with our own things. And Mom thinks it will smell fresher when we bake cookies. I hope they are both right because I don't want anybody visiting when our house smells like this!

Before we went upstairs, we all walked out to our backyard for the first time. At first, my heart shrunk. No flowers anywhere. No shed to keep our bicycles and lawnmower in. No swing set for Grace. No bird feeding station or birdbath. No clothesline for Mom. What kind of back yard is this anyhow?

But there is something here we never had before. In the very back of our yard is a grove of trees called Cherry Forest. Dad knows it's called that because he read it on a sign. So many trees! Dad says they belong to our house so we can play there.

John's eyes got as wide as a full moon on a starry night. He said, "You mean we can build forts there and make a zip line and collect lightning bugs in the summer?"

Dad nodded and said, "Well, yes, and no. Mom and I need to think about Cherry Forest before we say you can do anything you want. We will figure it out as a family, John. Let me just say Uncle Jim and I grew up with a woods near our house, and we had a blast collecting sticks and leaves to build bridges, forts, and animal shelters. We even made a bug hotel and a lookout tower."

Grandma chimed in, "Kids, your Dad and Uncle Jim always came home dirty and hungry from their time in the woods. You kids will love our little Cherry Forest, and I can't wait to see the array of birds that live here."

John said, "Maybe even owls, Grandma?"

"Oh, owls, yes! In fact, I read about the snowy owl who visits Maine in the winter. Wouldn't it be a hoot if a snowy owl came to Cherry Forest?"

Now all of this sounded good, but I wondered if Cherry Forest will be frightening at night. Will the trees bend and sway like monsters when it storms? What kind of bugs live there? Do other types of animals live there?

Dad says we will walk through Cherry Forest and make sure it's all very safe for our family. Grandma says, "I bet there are toads and wildflowers in the woods, kids! But watch out for poison ivy! Dad can show you what it looks like."

Mom says what she loves the most at our new house is the giant sugar maple tree that stands all by itself in the middle of our backyard. You can't miss it because it is smack dab in the middle.

Underneath the tree is a puddle of bright red and orange leaves that are deep enough to cover our shoes. I bet that's where we'll find Grace every day – playing in those leaves! John took no time climbing up the tree and swinging on the branches when Grandma cupped her hands around her mouth and shouted, "Be careful, John. We don't need a trip to the ER on our first day in our new home!" John rested in the crook of the branches.

Dad said we should consider ourselves incredibly lucky to have a sugar maple tree in our backyard.

He exclaimed, "Kids, sugar maples are a trademark of living in Maine! These trees put on a fantastic autumn show, as you see here. And maybe, just maybe, we can tap the tree and get maple syrup for our pancakes!"

What? We can get maple syrup from our back yard. I thought my legs would wobble from the very thought that this is possible. Will my friends in Nashville believe this?

Dad began sashaying around the maple tree, tapping his hand on his cheek like he does when he's thinking deeply.

Then he paced more and more around the tree - until out of the clear blue sky, he said the most amazing thing to us kids that made my ears believe angels were singing. He said, "Maybe, just maybe, next summer, we can build a treehouse with Uncle Jim's help. It's something I've always wanted to tackle."

Us kids gasped! Really, Dad, a treehouse?

Grandma declared to Mom, "Oh dear, there he goes blurting things out before he is 100% positive they can do it. I hope Dad and Jim CAN build a treehouse since Dad already let the cat out of the bag."

Mom agreed, "Me too, Grandma. Me too. Otherwise, may heaven help us next summer. The kids will never forget. Not even a small chance they won't bring it up again."

John asked, "Dad, can we watch that treehouse show on TV, and get ideas?"

"Sure, that's something we can do this winter to come up with some super cool plans for our treehouse!"

Grace asked, "Can we have lights on our treehouse, Dad?"

"Sure, that would make it even more amazing, Grace."

I said, "How about a rope swing and a tunnel or a water slide, Dad?"

"Whoa, kids. We don't even know we can build a treehouse yet. Something like this happens in steps, and we haven't taken the first baby step. We are merely thinking about this."

Mom and Grandma seemed concerned about something else. They huddled together, whispering something that Dad overheard. He said, "Don't you fret! Soon as we unpack the garage things, we'll put up our feeders and welcome the birds back. They will return without a shadow of a doubt. I'm so positive I'd bet my table saw on it."

Grandma looked relieved. She wondered, "Can we hang up the wind chimes on the front porch, too?"

Mom proclaimed, "Where's my clipboard? I have a list that will tell me which box has the wind chimes."

Grandma grinned and said, "Oh goody," as she clapped her hands.

I wondered about our long-lost birds in Tennessee because we always fed them and filled their birdbath with fresh water. Every single day. Dad gave them peanuts. Do you suppose the new family living in our old house is taking care of them? Or are the birds starving there?

Grandma keeps notes about birds in her bright blue spiral-bound bird-watching journal. She takes pictures of them with her binoculars camera and tapes the prints in her journal. Sometimes she even draws and colors them with colored pencils, then scribbles their scientific names in the journal.

I wished our new house would feel like home this very instant. I want it so bad; it hurts. I want everything to be unpacked and hung up like our old house: my shirts in the closet, our cookie jar in the kitchen, and our craft supplies in the cupboard.

Brown Creeper

They build nests in funny places.

smallish 4-6" long

brown & white

stiff tail

Certhia Americana

Spirals up tree trunks looking for bugs

INSECT EATER

LOVES BARK OF TREES

Spiral up the tree, little friend of mine

Brown Creeper

small songbird seen on Cedar tree in park. High-pitched and short call. September 27

Grandma says we will make this house our home in no time at all. I hope she's right because my heart is tangled up like a knot. The best and most perfect thing would be if we went back to our real home in Nashville.

I want Plan C.

CHAPTER 3:
NOTHING IS THE SAME

Nothing is the same here in Maple River. Some things are better, which I never expected, but some things are extra strange. I don't know why people don't talk about these weird things when they move.

For example, Maine is way colder than Tennessee. It's freezing here! The kids wear shorts and tee shirts, but they don't get goosebumps. Me? I shiver even in my red pants and long sleeve shirts in September.

Grandma proclaims, "The scent of the cool sea breeze is utterly refreshing." But kids my age don't care about sea breezes and things like that. At least I never thought about this stuff until Grandma pointed it out.

I didn't know how to turn the water on the first time I took a shower. I had to call my Mom into the bathroom to show me. At my old house, I swiveled the handle to the left, not quite all the way, and the warm water came out. But now I twist the hot and cold-water handles at the same time and then hold up on a little gizmo (what Grandma calls it) until the water comes out of the shower. Otherwise, the water fills the tub, and that's not what I want unless I'm taking a bath.

The light switches are all different, too. I keep reaching in the wrong place for the light switch when I go into my room. Mom tells me my brain just needs to adjust to the new way.

Even our kitchen wastebasket is in a new place. It used to be underneath our kitchen sink, which is precisely the right place for it. I keep opening the cupboard door under the sink, but it's not there.

"Molly Jo, it's not there anymore. Remember?"

"I know, Mom, I know." Grace says, "It's frustrating," and she's right.

Mom said, "I can think of one way you'll remember where the trash can is. Next time you have a wad of paper to throw away, let's see how far away you can throw it and make it into the basket!"

"Really, Mom?"

"Yes, let's turn it into a game of Paper Ball. I'd wager you won't ever look for it under the sink anymore." And she was right. I have the coolest Mom around.

I like my new bedroom, although it's smaller than the room Grace and I shared in Nashville. At our old house, Grace and I would slide my desk over to our window. At night, we'd perch there and gaze out watching the stars twinkle and airplanes buzz by.

On winter days, Grace and I used to blow on the windows to make steam on them and then draw pictures with our fingers and erase them with our nightgowns.

Here in our new bedroom, we have a giant window, and I'd love it if we could have a window bench. I just wished somebody, anybody, would realize how awesome that would be. I hoped to have my own room, but I didn't have a single flutter of hope.

Mom tells me, "You will get your own room someday, Molly Jo. And maybe even a window bench."

I know she wants that for me, but I'm not convinced it's ever going to happen.

"This year?"

"I don't exactly know," Mom told me with a lets-wait-and-see voice. "But until then, you will manage fine sharing your room with Grace. Try not to be too fussy."

I let out a huge sigh hoping she didn't hear me. She grew up with three brothers and a sister, and she never had her own room. Never ever in her whole life. Not even now!

Maybe Grace and I will always share a room. It's fine with me except when my friends come over. We older girls like to speak privately.

I asked Mom, "May I decorate my room how I want, Mom?"

"Sure, you and Grace can decide. She will like what you like. You're the big sister, so you're in charge."

Good! I want to spread my new red and yellow quilt on my bed, which Grandma sewed for me. I'd like a few grown-up things like a giant black and white clock on the wall and Dad's lava lamp on my desk. I hope we can get new stars for our ceiling, too.

Grace and I both like the large closet we have in our new room. My parents call it a walk-in closet. It's big enough to be a room. I could push my desk in there, or we could move both our beds in there.

If you want to know the real and exact truth, all I can think about is my old house. I remember running up my old stairs, belly-flopping on my bed, and waiting for Melissa to come over with a pile of books to read together.

Grandma says it takes time for a new place to become home. More than a few days. Mom and Dad are going to hang pictures soon, and that should help. I hope it doesn't take too long for this house to feel like home because my heart is continuously waiting for that good feeling.

How long will it take? Two days, two weeks, a year?

CHAPTER 4:
MAIL FROM MELISSA

Grandma said, "Molly Jo, Molly Jo, Molly Jo!"

"Uh, what Grandma?"

"You seem a million miles away. Have you been daydreaming?"

"I must have been, Grandma," I said, yawning, but with my mouth closed.

"You have a package from Melissa in the mail today. It is stamped 'private,' so I know it's meant only for you."

"Oh, let me see!" as she handed me the package with both hands. I secretly hoped Melissa would send me a letter, and she did.

"Why don't you take a few minutes and open the package in your room?" Grandma said.

"You don't mind, Grandma?"

"No," she said chuckling. "A girl needs her privacy sometimes. Head up to your room and take your time."

I wished that John would have received mail from one of his buddies, too. He doesn't seem to mind, especially since he likes living here. I think it's Cherry Forest he loves the most. I took Melissa's package to my room and flopped on my bed. The address label on the packaging says,

To: Molly Jo Daisy
154 Pine Grove Drive
Maple River, Maine

36

I still can't believe I live in Maine. My brain knows it's true, but my heart doesn't realize it yet.

I ripped open Melissa's package, pulled out a blue envelope, and a small box wrapped in bright green and yellow paper. Melissa sealed the back of the blue envelope with a wax seal that had a fancy "M".

I love wax seals! Grandma told me they were used a long time ago to keep letters very private; if the wax seal was broken, you know someone tampered with it. Inside the envelope was a two-page handwritten letter from Melissa on stationery with butterflies, so I began reading…

Dear Molly Jo,

I miss you so much. It's not the same without you here in Nashville. You probably know this is Melissa writing.

I have Mr. Emery for 5th grade. He loves to tell us funny stories. Today he told us about his little boy, Billy, who is an escape artist. Billy figured out how to climb out of his crib, crawl to the kitchen, open the refrigerator, and get himself a snack. One day he cracked eggs on the floor, and their dog ate them. Another time he put meatballs in their puppy's dog dish.

Remember when you would spend the night at my house, and we giggled so much that my Dad would knock on the door and tell us to be quiet? I miss those fun days, Molly Jo. You're my best friend and always will be.

Next page ---->

I wish you were still living across the street from me. Everyone here has asked about you and your family. They cannot believe you moved all the way to Maine. But I tell them it's not that far. We both see the same moon!

I made you this. Open it now. I hope you keep it forever.

By the way, how is it in Maine? I want to know all about it and all about your room. How's Grace? Is she doing okay? Does she carry Smokey around all the time like I thought she would? Is John finding new bugs and rocks in Maine to collect?

Write me back, please. And tell Grandma Banana I am learning to sew and that I love the pillow she made me. So far, I've made a few small bean bags.

I love you.
xoxo
Melissa

I put her letter down to open the little gift that's tied with a shiny yellow ribbon.

The gift card says: "To Molly Jo. Love Melissa. Just so that you don't forget where you used to live".

I unwrapped her gift, and wow! She made the outline of Tennessee in string art with little gold nails.

I would never forget where I used to live because I've spent my whole life there, but it's so neat that Melissa made this for me. She even has a heart on it right where Nashville is.

Right now, a giant lump is filling my throat, and the tears from my eyes are dripping on my quilt like a summer shower. I hope Melissa knows I love her right back. I really hope she knows.

I ran down the stairs, hugging the letter and string art under my arm to show Grandma and Mom.

"How is she, Molly Jo?" asked Grandma.

"Melissa misses me like I miss her. And nobody understands why we moved to Maine."

"Molly Jo, people move every day of the week. It was just our turn."

"Our turn, Grandma? I don't like being the quote-unquote new kid," I said sharply but wished I hadn't. "Melissa is never ever going to move."

Grandma said, "Well, maybe, and maybe not, but we never know what's in store for us. Who knows? You might meet the boy you will marry right here in Maple River."

"Oh, Grandma, that's so ridiculous. I don't even like boys!"

Grandma just smiled. "You're probably right, Molly Jo. That was plain ridiculous."

A boy from here would be so different. Wouldn't he? He would be from Maine. And that is so ridiculous to even consider living in Maine for the rest of my life.

I asked Grandma, "When someone asks me where I am from, what will I say?"

Grandma says, "You just tell them you're a girl with two hometowns. The next thing they will want to know is which two towns and you'll never run out of things to say."

Grandma believes she has everything figured out for me.

"Grandma, it will never be the same here in Maine."

She said, "Who needs the same? You will have to find the one thing."

What do you mean, the one thing?

"I mean, there must be one thing that made Nashville feel like home, and if you had that one thing here, you would feel at home here, too."

"How do I know what that one thing is, Grandma?"

"You just need to ask yourself a bunch of questions and figure it out, Molly Jo."

As I climbed the stairs back to my room, I wondered what that one thing could be.

CHAPTER 5:
DISCOVERING THE SECRET BOOK

You'd probably guess that Grace's and my room would be very tidy since we just moved here, but only half of our bedroom is neat, and it's my half. Grace is sloppy, and I don't mean that in a not-nice way. She just doesn't know how to fold shirts, line up books, and smooth her bedspread.

When we first arrived here, we emptied our moving boxes and put everything away in our dresser drawers. Grace likes to go fast, so she turned her boxes upside down and let everything land in her drawers. The first time she did it, I thought she was brilliant because the box was full of rolled-up socks. And they landed neatly in her drawer.

But the next box was packed with neatly folded shirts, that is, until she flipped it upside down on the floor, and everything came undone. So, she stuffed all her half-folded shirts into a crumpled wrinkly pile in her drawers. I couldn't believe it didn't even bug Grace one bit. How can she not care?

Her drawers are all jumbled up with socks, hair ties, friendship bracelets, quarters, nickels, spinners, and books. Her shirts are all wrinkly, and her pajamas are stuffed underneath her dresser in a pile. Every time she needs something, she has to fishing under there.

I can't take it any longer, so I told Mom and Grandma I would help Grace organize everything. The problem is that Grace will probably only help me for five minutes. That's what happens when you have a little sister.

Grace and I decided the best way to tackle our room is to start all over. We will take everything out of our drawers and off our shelves and put them in a big pile on our floor. Then we will sort through everything. But instantly, I realized my big mistake: we made a pile.

Have I told you that Grace likes to make piles? I am not kidding you. She has been doing this since she was just one year old. She makes piles of anything – toys, clothes, pillows, blankets, books. She pulls stuff from closets, out of drawers, and off the shelves. Then she makes big piles that become a twisted-spaghetti mess. And she never wants to return anything to where it belongs.

When Grace was tiny, we all thought this habit was cute. She was often sick, and nobody hollered at her about making piles of stuff. But now, now that she's four and doing much better, none of us, not even Grandma, laughs about it.

I was so wrong to suggest we dump everything in a pile. And now, in front of us is this giant crazy pile we need to tackle. What should we keep, and what should we toss? This is going to take a long time to go through. What did I get myself into?

Now and then, Grandma and Mom peeked in our room and shook their heads at the unsightly mess we created, but I hope we can surprise them with a clean room when we're done. Maybe it's the only way to make our sister space the way we want it.

I organized my old school papers into a tall, neat stack and decided to store them on our top closet shelf. That shelf is so high that I needed a stool to stand on. Grace handed me the papers, a small stack at a time. When I plopped them on the shelf, something was in the way.

44

I asked Grace to switch on the closet lights, and yes! There definitely WAS something in the way!

A book. A secret book with fancy printing on the cover. The title is *Advice for a Remarkable Life*. Wow, I want a remarkable life! Whose book is this? Maybe the people who used to live here left it behind by mistake.

I quickly glanced at a few pages inside. It's the skinniest chapter book I've ever seen.

"Grace, I found something special in our closet, but we cannot tell anybody."

"What is it, Molly Jo?"

"It's a book, Grace. And it's not just any book. It's a very secret book."

In her small voice, Grace said, "But why can't we tell anybody?"

"It's because this book is meant just for the two of us. Someone left it here for us. If we read it, we will have a Remarkable Life. It says so right on the cover. See? *Advice for a Remarkable Life.* Do you think it can be true? She nodded her head. "Yes, Molly Jo. I want a 'markable life!"

Right away, and I am not sure why, but I decided that we don't want John to see our book. He's smart without a doubt, but it takes courage and belief that a brother doesn't have.

"So, we have to hide it from him, Molly Jo?"

"Yes, we should have a good place to keep it. This book is for our eyes only, Grace."

"Can you read it to me at bedtime, Molly Jo?"

"Grace, it's not that kind of book with pictures and everything. Look and see - it's just plain words, but these are important words. No pictures or colors, no cartoons, just words."

"Okay," is all she said and shrugged her shoulders.

I set it back on the top shelf, way back in the corner. Nobody will ever find it there. After Grace goes to sleep tonight, I'll pull out my flashlight and read it from cover to cover.

If this book tells me how to have a remarkable life, this will be the best secret ever.

CHAPTER 6:
BEDTIME AND THE BOOK

Nighttime is hard on all of us because Grace has been a cry baby. I just want to plug my ears for all her sulking. I wished I could stay in Grandma's bedroom for now until Grace settles.

Every night, this is how it goes: Mom or Dad reads Grace a bedtime story, but then she cries for more. One more story. One more drink of water. One more bathroom visit. It's all a show.

Why is she suddenly behaving like a baby? She wasn't a cry baby at our old house. Grandma thinks her crying is because Grace is adjusting just like me. Grandma says Grace follows my lead, that I am her role model. Yikes!

Last night Grace cried for 20 minutes before falling asleep. Grandma is smart because she knows to stay in her own room with the door shut and her radio playing. John stays in his room, too. Neither of them must listen to Grace's crying.

I've thought about this a great deal, and tonight, I will try something new with Grace if Mom and Dad say it's okay. I don't know if it will work, but I think it's worth a try.

I'll make bedtime passes for her. At my old school, we used passes, and they worked with the kids. I will make three passes for Grace's bedtime. One for a bedtime story, one for a drink, and one for the bathroom. When the passes are gone, then it's time for her to go to sleep.

I'll explain to Grandma about the passes and get her thoughts.

Tonight, after Grace falls to sleep, I want to read that secret book we found. The one with the advice in it. I want my room to be silent, so nobody comes in to check on Grace. I have no idea what Mom and Dad would say about this book anyhow.

"I know how to get Grace to stop fussing at bedtime, Grandma."

"You'll be the family hero if you knew how to do that, Molly Jo."

"Well, it will be easy, Grandma."

"Keep talking."

"I made passes for Grace, and when she runs out of passes, it's time for her to go to sleep. It will be fun for her because I will explain that this is what big kids do at school!"

"Well, it's the best plan I've heard so far. Let Mom and Dad know and see if they agree."

Mom and Dad jumped on the idea and told me that I could tell Grace about it. Even John thought it was a "super-duper idea," using his own words.

So, after dinner, I sat down with Grace and explained the whole game. She will get three bedtime passes, and once they are all used up, it's time to go to sleep. Grace hopped up and down and said she couldn't wait for bedtime.

She wanted to use the passes right away, but I told her we must wait till 8:00 tonight – that's rule #1. You can't begin before bedtime.

At 8:00 pm, I gave the three passes to Grace. She studied them hard and said she wanted to use two passes. I said,

"Two! That's fine, but once the passes are gone, then it's time for bed."

"I know, Molly Jo. I know all about that. You told me that already."

Grace gave Mom the pass for a bedtime story and a drink of water. Mom read her a short bedtime story, and then got her a glass of water and told her it was bedtime.

Grace said, "But I have one more pass."

Mom said, "Okay, it says bathroom. Take a quick trip and come right back."

Grace ran into the bathroom and did her job, and then ran back to her bed. Mom tucked her into bed and turned out the lights.

She said, "We can play this game again tomorrow night, Grace."

Grace didn't whimper. Not one teeny bit.

She climbed into her cozy bed with piles of pillows, grabbed Smokey, nuzzled him against her neck, and her blankets up under her chin, and shut her eyes. And within a few minutes, she slept like a baby. I couldn't believe it myself. She has cried at bedtime every night since we left Nashville, and now, she's sound asleep.

Mom and Dad high-fived me. John hugged me, and so did Grandma. I never guessed this would work with Grace, but now that it did, I'm thinking I could sell this idea to parents!

Grandma said, "Now you're using your powers, Molly Jo."

When I knew that Grace was sleeping for the night, I got my blue flannel pajamas on, brushed my teeth, and said goodnight to everyone. Dad said, "So early? Molly Jo, it's not like you to be so prompt to bed. Are you feeling alright?"

"I feel fine, Dad. Just tired!" as I tried to fake-yawn.

"That's good, Molly Jo, because you need to start going to bed earlier since school starts the day after tomorrow. And remember, you and John are doing a practice bus run tomorrow morning, so you have to rise and shine early!"

"I know, Dad. I know."

As I tiptoed into my room with a tiny flashlight, being careful not to wake up Grace, I pulled that secret book out from under my top shelf in the closet. It's finally time. This could be the beginning of something big.

I don't know why I think this, but I believe the best secrets in the whole world might be right here in this book of mine.

I wonder if other people know about this book and why someone left it here. I wonder if the family who left this house is searching for it. Or maybe it belonged to one of their kids, and the parents didn't even know about it.

I'm glad I remembered my flashlight. I made a tent out of my sheets so I can sit up and read my book. I settled in and opened the book.

Inside the front cover, there's a handwritten note that says, "To Christopher from Mr. Simmons. Use this book wisely and see what happens. And remember, never ever give up."

See what happens? What could possibly happen? And I wonder who Mr. Simmons is. Maybe he was Christopher's teacher, whoever Christopher is. I have so many questions. This is driving me crazy.

The book is small, so maybe I can read the whole thing tonight. That would be perfect. So, I began leafing through it and saw chapters like these...

- Learn Fun and Handy Things

- Hang Out with Really Good People

- Mistakes are Awesome

- You Already Have What You Need

- Happiness Is Your Decision

Well, I didn't expect these kinds of things in this book, but I started reading the first chapter...

Learn Fun and Handy Things
Advice for a Remarkable Life

When the opportunity arises for you to learn something fun or handy, just take the time to do it because those little things will become big things as you get older. If someone offers to teach you how to make an omelet or a milkshake, do it! If you get to learn how to tie different kinds of knots or paint a room, do it!

Do you realize that knowing how to do things for yourself is powerful? You don't have to ask or hire someone, and you can dazzle your family with your knowledge. And maybe you can even earn money from things you know how to do.

If you can fix a squeaky door, use a sewing machine, or put air in your tires, then bravo for you! If you can chop vegetables, make a pie, put up a tent, cast a reel, or build a birdhouse, you can be proud of yourself.

Learn fun skills too! You could learn to juggle, read super-fast, walk on stilts, blow giant bubbles, or do magic tricks. Practice playing spoons and entertain your friends. Get to know a few card games, a few board games, and a yard game or two.

You'll be further ahead than many adults if you know how to cook a few dishes, be handy with tools, and put smiles on faces. When someone offers to teach you something they know how to do, grab the opportunity. You won't ever regret knowing how to do something remarkable.

That's good advice. I have already learned a lot of things from Grandma. Still, I wish this book explained how to convince my parents to move back to Nashville or get Melissa's family to come to Maple River.

Did Christopher, whoever-he-is, leave this book behind by accident? Or did he leave it here on purpose, hoping Grace and I would find it?

I genuinely wanted to read the whole book, but I couldn't keep my eyes open for being so sleepy. So, I slid the book under my pillow, hoping to read more tomorrow night.

The cold September rain crackled as it hit my window. Our big oak tree in the front yard swayed back and forth like a giant monster, casting big shadows across my quilt. I wasn't scared, well, maybe a little, so I wrapped my pillow around my ears, pulled my quilt under my chin, and then...I must have drifted to sleep.

CHAPTER 7:
SILLY TRIAL BUS RUN

The next morning, I was so bleary-eyed, I could hardly wake up for the sleepiness in my eyes. I thought I heard sizzling bacon downstairs, or so I thought. Ack! It's cars buzzing by on the wet street. Oh no, make it not so. I wish the rain would go away.

On mornings like this, my body is so relaxed, so totally melted into my bed that I must wiggle my fingers and toes to know where they even are. I absolutely, positively, didn't want to get up on this dark, rainy morning, but Mom called my name.

"Molly Jo, it's time to get up! We're doing a practice run for the school bus. I know you're sleepy, but this is no time to hurkle-durkle."

I wish she didn't say "hurkle-durkle." Those words bug me. Grace was already up, playing with Smokey in her bed.

My sleepy eyes snapped open. I dragged myself out of bed, brushed my teeth with my eyes closed, buttoned my penguin shirt, and nearly crawled downstairs, where I heard Grandma setting the table for breakfast. She had cereal and juice out for John and me, but even the thought of eating cereal made my stomach do flip flops.

Mom said, "Molly Jo, even though this is just a practice run, I want you to eat a little something before running down the street for the bus. And check out the buttons on your shirt - the penguins aren't lined up."

I guess I missed a buttonhole.

John was eating a big bowl of crispy rice flakes and playing a maze on the back of the cereal box. The table was shaking because of John wiggling his legs – all the time. Why can't he just be still for once? Please?

This whole thing seemed so silly to me. Getting up early on a dark rainy day and running down the street to catch a bus that isn't even coming. Nobody else in the ENTIRE world will be doing this. And I hope nobody notices us out there.

Like every other morning, Grandma scrambled Grace some cheesy eggs, made her peanut butter toast, and said, "Cut on the dotted line." Grandma cuts Grace's toast into two triangles, but she doesn't cut all the way through so that Grace can pull the triangles apart herself. Grandma used to do that to my toast too.

Mom told John and me, "You only have five minutes before you need to be outside. And it's still raining, so make sure you're prepared."

She even packed lunches for us because she wanted a trial run on packing lunches too. That's silly because packing lunches isn't anything new.

When it was time for us to leave the house, we put on our rain jackets, and Mom gave us our lunches to take with us. This is going to look ridiculous, standing on the dark sidewalk in the rain, waiting for a bus that isn't coming, and carrying a lunch that we will eat at home. Mom said she would go with us, which makes things even worse!

So, Mom, John, and I scrambled out the front door in an "imaginary hurry," carrying our brown bag lunches and umbrellas. Mom says, "The bus will pick you up at the corner house, three doors down. The house with the big blue porch."

We waited in the rain a few minutes for imaginary bus #94 to "pick us up" and then ran home with our slightly wet brown bag lunches. Mom took her time walking back in the light rain, as John and I raced to our porch and back inside our cozy house.

We tore off our wet rain jackets, hung them on the hooks, and sat down at the table with our brown lunch bags. We both knew it wasn't lunchtime, but neither of us wanted to wait to eat what Mom packed. So, we pulled everything out of our bags. My lunch had mandarin oranges, cheese crackers, and a salami sandwich with mustard. My favorite!

John's lunch was the same, but he also had olives that I absolutely hate, but he absolutely loves. Mom says I shouldn't say the word hate, so I will do better. I totally do not like olives as much as I totally do not like peas. And that's a proven fact.

Mom walked into the house with a surprised look on her face when she saw that we were ripping into our lunches. She shook her head but then didn't say a word, so John and I resumed and enjoyed every bite. That should make her happy, right?

The rest of the day, Grace and I played together in our room, and I found myself dreading tomorrow. Maybe dreading isn't the right word, but I was not looking forward to the first day of school.

I really wish I could be excited like I would have been in Nashville. I am trying to think good thoughts as Grandma tells me, but my head is interrupted by worries:

Nobody is going to know me.

Won't everybody else already have friends?

Will I be able to find my classroom?

Who will have lunch with me?

Why did we have to move to here anyhow?

Thinking of the first day of school is The First Worst.

CHAPTER 8:
MY FIRST MORNING AT SCHOOL

Morning came again, and it was still raining and dark outside. Eww! I was glad that John and I did a trial run of the bus yesterday because it will seem easier today. I AM the big sister, even though John sometimes figures things out before me.

From our breakfast table, we could hear the rumbling of the school bus and the squeaky brakes stopping and starting way down the street. John and I threw on our rain jackets, grabbed our backpacks, and ran out the front door shouting bye to everybody. I didn't know whether I should feel excited or exasperated. I think Mom planned on coming out to the bus with us, but it all happened so fast!

The morning was still dark. While trampling through the soggy wet leaves on the sidewalk, I accidentally stepped into a very deep puddle. Ack! I should have worn my rain boots as Mom said, but nobody wears rain boots in fifth grade!

Now water is squirting out the sides of my shoes every single step I take. I really wanted to run back home, but I had no time. I wish I could have hidden in my bed for the whole entire day.

The bus pulled up, and the bus door opened. Our bus driver, Mr. Kim, greeted us with a big smile. For a moment, I almost forgot it was a dark, rainy morning. He quickly looked at his clipboard and said, "Good Morning Millie Jo and John." I was surprised he knew our names, except my name isn't Millie Jo.

He said," Oops, I meant Molly Jo. I have a granddaughter named Millie, so I hope you forgive me for mixing up your name with hers."

I didn't mind. I didn't mind at all. Maybe I'll change my name to Millie Jo when I grow up.

The bus was nearly full, but John and I found seats together. Everyone was quiet; I think the kids must be sleepy.

Mr. Kim shouted out, "Welcome to my bus! What's the word of the day?"

"Word of the day?" I wondered.

"It's brouhaha," John shouted out. "Brouhaha is the word of the day."

Mr. Kim said, "Aha! I like that, John. If the varsity team loses their football game, I am certain we will have a brouhaha."

How does John know this word? What made him speak up on his very first day on the bus? Even I don't understand what brew-ha-ha is. It scrambles my mind.

The rest of our ride was still and quiet except for the rattling bus. When we pulled up to our new school, Maple River Elementary, just about everyone hurried off the bus knowing precisely what to do and where to go. John and I had a vague idea because Mom and Dad took us on a tour of the school a few days ago, but it all looks different to me this morning.

The hallways were crowded with kids chatting with their friends. Without any confusion or worry, John went on his merry way to his classroom. But as I watched him go down his hallway, I noticed he stopped and twisted around to look for me.

He ran over to me, catching his breath, and said, "You know where your classroom is, don't you, Molly Jo?"

"Of course, I do," realizing I wasn't 100% sure.

He said, "Great, because there's enough time for me to run down there with you."

And so, we hurried down my hallway, the opposite direction of where John's classroom is. He saw my classroom door with the colorful peacock on it and said, "Oh, there it is, Molly Jo." And then it clicked. Yes, it's the door with the painted peacock. We are going to be learning about exotic birds.

He peeked his head inside my classroom, looked for about two seconds, and said, "Gotta scoot. See you after school, Molly Jo." And off he went down the hall toward his own classroom on the other end of our school.

I think John has a built-in map on his forehead because he finds his way around places. I wished I had a map on my forehead as he does, then my stomach wouldn't feel so queasy about my new school. I am glad John helped me this morning without bragging.

When I stepped into my classroom, my teacher, Ms. Jewel, was busy sorting papers. She wore a stack of silver bracelets that made musical sounds when she moved her arm. When she noticed me, her face beamed like sunshine. I never saw a teacher's face do that as Ms. Jewel's does.

She glanced over her reading glasses and said, "Good morning, Molly Jo Daisy. I am so thrilled to meet you. I hear you've moved here all the way from Nashville! Wow! Was that your brother I saw peeking in? Tell him he can come back any time and stay awhile."

"Yes, that was him. He's a 3rd grader," I told Ms. Jewel.

I am so glad she knows my name already.

Ms. Jewel noticed that wherever I walked, my shoes were squirting water from the sides and making little puddles all over the floor.

"Oh, dear! You're making puddles, Molly Jo. Do you want some dry socks?"

"Uh, yes, Ms. Jewel. That would be good."

"Well, these socks may not be pretty, but they are clean and dry. I have them just in case anyone marches into a giant puddle!"

Wow, I couldn't believe it. Ms. Jewel handed me a towel and a pair of clean white socks with a plastic bag for my wet socks and told me I could change. I can't even begin to say how much better it feels having dry socks on. And then Ms. Jewel showed me to my desk, which is in the first row.

CHAPTER 9:
LUNCH, ANNA LIN, AND FISH

I t never dawned on me that there could be another new kid in my class, but there is because I could hear Ms. Jewel welcoming her. Her name is Anna Lin, and she has a red backpack like mine.

She is wearing a twirly skirt with ribbons, and sometimes I see her spinning around with the ribbons fluttering behind her. Grace would love wearing twirly skirts.

Maybe, just maybe, Anna Lin and I could be lunch pals today. She probably doesn't have any friends yet either.

After everybody figured out where they sit in the classroom, Ms. Jewel explained the rules. The most important thing she said is that fifth graders have more rights than any other class at Maple River Elementary because we're the oldest. But we only get to keep our privileges if we follow the rules. Now I kind of wished I didn't sit in the front row. Not that I break the rules, but maybe I bend them, once in a while. She told us she won't put up with shenanigans, whatever that means.

Ms. Jewel allowed each of us kids in the class to stand up, tell our name, and something we did over the summer. I was the only one who said I spent my summer in Nashville with my best friend, Melissa. Ms. Jewel stuck a pin on a map where Nashville is and said our class will learn about Tennessee.

She said I could lead the lesson and tell the class what it was like to live there. That's good because then I can tell my class how life in Tennessee is better than living here. At least for me.

When the other new girl, Anna Lin, said that she was from Caribou, Maine, Ms. Jewel stuck a pin on the map where Caribou is.

Ms. Jewel said, "Goody, next week, our brand-new students, Anna Lin and Molly Jo, can tell us about their hometowns!"

And she asked for two volunteers to tell about what it's like to live in Maple River. One boy, Jeffrey, and one girl, Charlotte, were selected.

I never knew things would move so fast on the first day. I already have an assignment for next week.

It's 11:00 and lunch is only twenty minutes away. I haven't asked Anna Lin to eat lunch with me yet because there was no time. Between all the homeroom rules, social studies, and now my favorite class, language arts, our morning has been filled.

Will Anna Lin have a friend to eat lunch with? Or would she rather eat by herself? She probably doesn't realize I want to be her friend because she's a new kid too. I could wait till tomorrow to ask her.

The buzzer rang, and everyone jumped to their feet. I got my lunch bag, and I saw Anna Lin getting hers. Ms. Jewel told us to get in line by the door so that we can go to the cafeteria. There are two lines, the buyers, and the packers. Both Anna Lin and I are packers.

I tried to get in line right behind Anna Lin, but two other kids jumped in front of me, and now she is three people ahead of me. We strolled down to the cafeteria, and Ms. Jewel says that our class should stay at the two tables by the window overlooking the garden.

On the other side of the cafeteria, I saw John sitting with one of his classmates. John is such a goofy brother, making funny faces at the other kids and whooping up a storm. I can't imagine acting silly like that at school, but John doesn't care what people think.

Anna Lin sat alone at the end of a table. I wondered if I should take a seat next to Anna Lin. Will she think I am bothering her?

She seems like someone nice, so I edged over closer to her and noticed a tiny smile suddenly appear.

She said, "Hi, Molly Jo."

Oh wow, she knows my name!

I asked, "Are you eating with anyone, Anna Lin?"

"No, but you can have lunch with me if you want, Molly Jo."

So, I took the seat beside her. And for a moment there was nothing but silence. My mind searched for something to say. I wish I could think of something, anything. But no words came to me. What kind of girl can't think of a single word to say?

Anna Lin reached into her lunch box and pulled out a ham sandwich with curly lettuce peeking out between the bread. Then she reached in and pulled out something else: a deck of cards. I wondered what in the world, but before anything else could come out of my mouth, she said, "You want to play Fish?"

"Fish? What do you mean?"

"You know, the card game."

"Oh, yes. I like that game," I said although I hadn't played Fish since I was six.

Anna Lin explained, "The kids at my old school played Fish every day, and so I thought maybe the kids here would like it too."

So, we started eating our sandwiches, and Anna Lin dealt the cards. Before we knew it, three other kids in our class were standing over us, wondering if they could play. Maybe it's more fun than I imagined.

Anna Lin asked the other kids, "Wanna play?"

"Yeah, can we?"

"Sure, have a seat, and I'll deal your cards." And so, they sat down, and the five of us played as if we'd known each other.

I don't know how Anna Lin realized that playing Fish was a good idea, but it made lunch fun, and neither of us felt alone.

Even the kids who weren't new wanted to play with us. Anna Lin is fun!

When I got home that day, I was super tired! Mom says it's because it was the first day of school, which takes LOTS of energy. She said I might feel that way for the first week or two, but then it will seem like I've always been there. I hope I do!

Mom and Grandma made salad, crunchy chicken strips, and baked potatoes with bacon bits for dinner. Dad suggested we go around the table and share something that made us happy today, especially on our first day of school in Maple River. We call it Simple Joys.

We always did Simple Joys at our house in Nashville, but we forgot to start it back up here in Maple River – until today when Dad remembered. He said that the first day of school is something to celebrate.

John said, "My simple joy is the word of the day. Brouhaha! Mr. Kim and I like it!"

Dad said, "What does brouhaha mean, John?"

"Mr. Kim said it's something about football, Dad. Not quite sure. I just know I like that word."

"Maybe you can look it up after dinner and tell the whole family exactly what it means. Oh, and you, Grace? What's your Simple Joy today?"

"It's the big pile of stuff on our bedroom floor that Molly Jo dropped there."

Me. Sigh. Both of us put it there.

"And you, Grandma?"

"I found my lemongrass and spearmint tea at the market today. It's the one thing that lets me know I'm truly at home now."

Mom said, "My Simple Joy today was having a quiet, normal day and getting a good report about Grace from the doctor."

Knowing that Grace is doing well puts a smile on ALL our faces, but why in the world would having a normal day be a Simple Joy?

Dad said, "My Simple Joy is officially working with Uncle Jim at Daisy Designs. I didn't realize how good this would be for our family."

And then it was my turn.

I said, "My Simple Joy was Fish."

Nobody understood what I was meaning, so I had to explain about playing Fish at lunchtime today. John wondered if he could join us the next time we played.

Dad says, "Well, maybe you could take a deck of cards to school and play with your classmates, John."

John said, "Or maybe I could organize a no-blinking contest."

"No-blinking contest?" said Dad.

"Yes, Dad, I heard there are some people who can go for over an hour without blinking. That would be fun to try."

"Your lunch break isn't that long, John. I think you better stick to playing cards or drawing. Forget the blinking, no-blinking thing. You're wiser than that. Blinking is a good thing, John. Maybe you can research that, too."

For my first day at school in Maine, I am a little surprised it was better than I expected, but I still wished I could be at my old school where I know everybody and don't have to start all over. Ack!

The First Worst day is over. I made it, but to be fair, I should give it a better name.

Hang Out with Really Good People
Advice for a Remarkable Life

You may not yet realize, but the friends you choose make a huge difference in your life.

Why does it matter who your friends are? Your circle of friends matters because the more you hang out with your friends, the better chance you will become like them. And they will become like you. So, choose the best friends you can!

Have you ever watched your Mom or Dad make a pot of soup? Before they put the ingredients into the pan, like the carrots, chicken, peas, and potatoes, each of those ingredients had their own distinctive flavor. But after they simmer in the soup together, the flavors mingle, and that's why soup is so good!

Your friends are kind of like that soup. When you're together, you will make each other even better. Now, if you add something yucky to the soup, like a rotten potato, all the soup would soon taste bad.

Instead of hanging around people who bring you down or make fun of you, find friends who appreciate you, have good ideas and inspire you. When you are in a pickle (a not so good situation), it REALLY helps to have supportive friends who lift you up, help you do the right thing, and believe in you.

A quality circle of friends is one of the **best gifts** you can give yourself.

CHAPTER 10:
LEARNING THE UPSIDE-DOWN WAY

After school the next day, John and his new friend William were doing art homework at the kitchen table. I couldn't believe John already has friends over. And William seems nice too. Why am I not that lucky?

What they were doing seemed funny to me, and yet I was curious. John's art teacher gave them a picture of a cocker spaniel for them to draw. But instead of drawing it the usual way, their assignment is to stare at the cocker spaniel upside down and then draw it. And they are not supposed to turn their drawing around until they are all the way finished.

Why would the teacher expect the kids to draw something upside down? That seems hard!

John said, "Mr. Gregory told us that if we try to draw pictures the normal way, our brains think it's hard like we can't do it. But if we draw the same thing by looking at it upside down, it's just like drawing lines and dots, and curves and it's easier."

William said, "Yeah, we are tricking our brains into thinking this is easy."

Oh. That makes sense! Maybe I'll try it for myself later when they are not watching me.

I heard them telling each other not to peek until their pictures were finished. But William could see John's drawing, and John could see William's drawing.

When they shifted their pictures around, they both had astonished wide-eyed looks on their faces and made big "ooh" sounds. Drawing upside down worked! John says his drawing turned out better than when he draws the right side up.

"I wonder if there are other fun things to do upside down."

William says, "Yeah, I wonder too. What if we did our math homework upside down? It wouldn't work though because the 6's would look like 9's and the 7's would look like L's."

And John added, "And the 3's would look like fancy E's. "

I secretly wished Melissa could come over, but she's over a thousand miles away. John is always super lucky about things.

When I asked Grandma, she said, "Molly Jo, you have superpowers. You just need to use them. Someone out there is needing a friend, and you could be that person."

Grandma went on to say, "Remember, Molly Jo, your brother was excited about coming to Maine."

"Yeah, but he wasn't as sad about leaving as me, Grandma. I had to leave Melissa."

"Well, you're right, Molly Jo, but John has friends he misses too. He looks at things a little differently, and that helps him more than you realize. Don't you remember as soon as he knew we'd be moving, he started dreaming about the neat things he would find here?"

"I know that, Grandma," I said with my hands on my hips.

"Sometimes you can learn a lot from your little brother. I know he annoys you, and he is messy as all get out, but he has a way of turning lemons into lemonade."

"He is always messy, Grandma. Have you seen his room?"

"Focus on his good points because he does that for you, Molly Jo."

Grandma is right, and I wished I had used my brain. I'm the big sister, and I could feel my face getting warmer and warmer.

"John learns from you, Molly Jo. He's proud of you as a big sister. He thought your cookie project was the best when you baked cookies and took them to sick kids at the hospital."

"Maybe I can do something like that here in Maple River, Grandma."

"Explore your new world here with your sparkly eyes and come up with an idea to spread your magic in Maple River."

"Okay, Grandma," I said. "What could it possibly be? I don't even know my way around here yet."

Grandma said, "I know moving has been hard on you, Molly Jo. It's not your fault, but this move is a blessing, an opportunity, an adventure! Now that we are here in Maine, you can be sad and mad or be brave and excited. You can choose."

Could it really be that easy? I never heard Grandma explain it this way before, but she's right. Come to think of it, I do know someone from school - Anna Lin! She seems nice. Maybe she wants a friend like I do; I'm done with aloneness.

Mistakes Are Awesome
Advice for a Remarkable Life

Mistakes aren't bad, so don't be afraid to make them. After all, it means you are trying, and it is way better than doing nothing. One good thing about making errors is that you will learn from them and try a different way next time.

Suppose you forget to put the milk back in the refrigerator, and it became sour. You probably won't do that again because sour milk tastes yucky. Have you ever accidentally left your wallet at the store? Oh, no! You'll be more careful next time. Maybe your neighbor paid you to pull weeds, but they grew right back because you didn't pull out the whole root. Argh!

Have you ever left your chocolate bar in the sun, and it melted? Or called a friend by the wrong name?

Throughout your life, you will make many mistakes in what you say, in your schoolwork, and in other surprising ways. It's alright. What is important is that you learn from your mistakes. Fix them and keep going. Mistakes lead to success!

Do you know about Thomas Edison, the famous American inventor? One of his many inventions was an improved filament for the electric light bulb, the part that makes the light in the bulb.

He tried many ways to get it right, but he never gave up. He didn't look at his mistakes as failures, but rather just ways that didn't work. So, do your best, but don't be discouraged when you make mistakes.

Sometimes the best things come from a "mistake" like chocolate chip cookies. Look it up and you will see.

CHAPTER 11:
A LESSON I WON'T EVER FORGET

The next afternoon, when I got home from school, Grandma was sitting on the couch, folding a basket of clean laundry. I plopped down beside her and buried my nose in the laundry basket, sniffing in the fresh smell of the towels and pajamas that just came out of the dryer.

Grandma said, "Molly Jo, if you have time to smell the clean laundry, then you can help me fold."

I told Grandma that I had something important to tell her about school, and she tossed some clothes onto my lap to fold. Then she said, "I'm all ears, Molly Jo. But instead of folding, why don't we go out on the porch, and you can tell me about your school day."

That sounds way better than folding clothes. So out the squeaky screen door we went, and we rocked back and forth on our porch swing. I told Grandma about the first day of school when Ms. Jewel stuck a pin on the map where we used to live and that I will be doing a presentation to our class about Nashville.

Grandma remarked, "That's genuinely nice that Ms. Jewel is honoring where you used to live. Not all teachers do that."

"Well, it seems complicated. I don't know what I will even talk about, Grandma. And another new girl, Anna Lin, is going to be telling the class about where she used to live, too."

"How nice there's another new girl. Maybe you two can become friends! Did Ms. Jewel tell you she would ask you a lot of questions about Tennessee?"

"No, she didn't, Grandma. But I just know she will."

Grandma chuckled. "You worry a bit too much, Molly Jo."

Maybe I do know a few things about Tennessee. I know the capital is Nashville and that it's a southern state and that it doesn't get as cold as Maine.

"Molly Jo, you know tons of things about Nashville! Maybe you can write down some fun facts to tell your class. What are some things that are different between Tennessee and Maine? Between Nashville and Maple River? Kids like knowing what's different, don't they?"

"I guess they do, Grandma."

"Some children in your class probably never tried moon pies or went to a meat and three," said Grandma. "And you could tell them about the Steeplechase in the spring."

"That's funny, Grandma. I thought everyone has eaten moon pies and been to a meat and three."

"You think that because you're used to those things, Molly Jo. They are commonplace in your world. Maybe you could figure out the difference between moon pies and whoopie pies."

I told Grandma, "Maybe I can also tell my class about the Parthenon. I did a report back in Nashville about how it's the same size and shape as the Parthenon in Greece. A replica."

"Remember, you're the expert, Molly Jo. What you share will probably be new knowledge to the kids here in Maine. They will be all ears, so you will have their attention."

"Okay, Grandma, maybe I can tell my class how it's BETTER living in Tennessee than in Maine."

"My heavens, that would NOT BE NICE," Grandma said with a cross face I've never seen on her. Her frown lines popped out between her eyebrows, and her eyes stared straight into mine.

Then she said, "This is a good time for a lesson, dear girl. Please get your Dad's shaving cream from the bathroom and meet me in the kitchen."

My heart melted into my stomach, but I did as Grandma told me and got the shaving cream from the medicine cabinet. Grandma marched into the kitchen and pulled out a big silver bowl from the cupboard and plunked it squarely on the kitchen table.

She said, "Now, dear girl, squirt the whole can of shaving cream into this bowl."

The whole can? I did what Grandma wanted me to do even though my chin was quivering.

"Keep going," she said, tapping her finger on the table. "Squirt the whole can into the bowl."

I must have said the wrong thing. I know I did.

"Alright, Molly Jo. Now that the bowl is filled up with shaving cream, I want you to put it all back into the can."

"Put it back? Really, you want me to put it back. I can't do it. There's no way, Grandma," I blurted out with my shaky voice.

I knew I couldn't. That would be impossible.

Grandma sat down, and her face became much softer as she patted the chair beside her and asked me to sit down.

She said, "I love you, sweet girl. Please always remember that your words are like shaving cream. Once they are out of your mouth, you cannot take them back. Your words matter, Molly Jo. They matter greatly, so choose your words with great care.

"Believe me, I am not an angel myself. Sometimes I say things I wish I could take back. But I want you to remember the shaving cream and always remember that your words have power. It's not kind to say that Tennessee is better than Maine. The children here are immensely proud to be from Maine.

"I know you love where we used to live, but have you given Maple River a chance? Even you said that Maple River is a super cute town. And you love blueberry pie – Maine is the place where blueberries are grown! PLUS Ms. Jewel has welcomed you with open arms at your school. That's something to celebrate."

"Sorry, Grandma, I lost my head when I said that Tennessee is better than Maine. Both places are good, right?"

Grandma said, "You can be proud of being from both places. From the Grand Ole Opry to the beautiful rocky Maine coast, you are one blessed girl. You're welcome to have your own opinions, Molly Jo, but do so with kindness. Naturally, you treasure your home in Nashville, but I believe Maple River will also steal your heart."

I took a deep breath and let it out sharply. I don't want to see the shaving cream come out again nor that look on Grandma's face. If Grandma hadn't called me out, I might have blurted out something stupid at school. I guess I haven't been very grown up about moving.

Grandma said, "Go easy on yourself, Molly Jo. Sometimes you let your emotions run over you like a truck tire on a tiny ant. You know, sweet girl, I am on your side. I am always on your side."

I knew Grandma meant that from her heart, which is comforting, but I need to shake off this fog of yucky feelings. *What I read from my secret book about learning from mistakes is true. Next time, I will think before I blurt out my words.* I should have already known that, but I will do better.

As I was about to head upstairs, I heard John tell Mom, "Grandma was a little hard on Molly Jo, don't you think?"

Mom said, "Yes, Molly Jo put a bee in Grandma's bonnet, but remember, Grandma is on Molly Jo's side. That was a lesson of love, John, and if you listened to any of it, you would have learned something important about the words you say."

As John poured a tall glass of milk, he said, "I'm not going to say another word ever!"

Mom just chuckled, and I noticed more of that gloom inside me melt away.

I trudged upstairs to my bedroom to unload my backpack and get myself discombobulated. I wanted to just chill for a little while, but when I plopped my school bag on my bed, something flashing on my bedroom wall caught my eye.

As I stared a little closer, I noticed a photo frame hanging there, something I'd never seen before. It's like a fantastic slide show with all sorts of pictures from our old house and our old friends. My eyes nearly traveled around my head – it's that wonderful!

One by one, pictures of Nashville, Melissa, and many good memories flashed by. I ran downstairs to tell Grandma and Mom all about it.

John shouted, "Did you see it, Molly Jo?"

"The photo frame? How do you know about it, John?"

"Do you like it? Dad and I put it up for you."

"Like it? I love it! Those pictures are the best memories."

Mom said, "John came up with the idea. Maybe when we visit Aunt Jane's house tomorrow, we will take some more pictures for your new photo frame. Do you like that idea, Molly Jo?"

I privately told Mom, "I believe it's the grandest idea, but what I'd really like to do is surprise John as he surprises me."

You Already Have What You Need
Advice for a Remarkable Life

How could we already have what we need? Perhaps you don't already have a new bike or pair of shoes that you want, but you have the essential ingredients to be a fantastic person.

You already have courage, integrity, and friends. You were born with problem-solving skills and a sense of humor. Just think how easily babies laugh, and how quickly they figure out how to get your attention.

If you believe that only other people have these things, you need to look inside yourself and find them because they are there. You may simply need to awaken them.

Have you ever looked at a forest, and all you can see is trees? That is until you look closer. If you were to walk into the woods, suddenly you would know that the forest is much more than just trees. The forest is home to woody vines and mosses clinging to rocks, tiny bugs, colorful birds, leaping frogs and playful squirrels, piles of acorns, and blankets of wildflowers.

When you look in the mirror, maybe all you see is the person you think you are. But what would it be like if you looked deep inside and found a toolbox with most everything you ever needed? A mind to figure things out, courage when you need it, strength to do the right thing, and friends. Yes, friends. Sometimes friends find us, and sometimes we find them.

Everything you need, you already have, right inside of you. If you haven't recognized that lately, it is time to awaken the gifts you already have.

CHAPTER 12:
VISITING AUNT JANE & UNCLE JIM'S HOUSE

B ack when we lived in Nashville, I never dreamed that we'd live close to Aunt Jane's and Uncle Jim's family. But now that we are here in Maple River, it's incredible that we can visit them and come back home all in the same day! Even in the same afternoon.

Since Dad works at Uncle's Jim's woodshop, he said Mom could drive us up and see where he works. And that means I also get to see cousin Claire and Aunt Jane. Mom and Grandma will drive us kids there after school.

As soon as John and I got off the bus and ran home, Mom was ready to go to Uncle Jim and Aunt Jane's. She covered a warm chocolate cake with tin foil, and Grandma's baked bean casserole was ready to go. I guess that means we are staying for dinner at Aunt Jane's! Hurray! Even better than I thought.

Grace brought Smokey, wrapped in a soft green blanket. John brought his cigar box of rocks, tightly closed with two rubber bands, and we all piled in the van with Mom and Grandma.

Mom thought she already knew the way to Uncle Jim's house, but on the way there, she forgot where to exit the roundabout for Uncle Jim's house. John and I snapped our mouths shut to keep from laughing because she kept going around and around. "Quiet," Mom said, shaking her head. "I've got to focus."

We all became silent because Mom's face meant business. She took the second right, and we were on our way.

Twenty-five minutes is all it takes from our house to Uncle Jim's house. When we pulled into Aunt Jane's driveway, Dad's pickup was parked there because this is where he works now. He still has Tennessee license plates, which makes us very cool. People probably can't believe we moved here from over 1,201 miles away. I can hardly believe it myself.

Aunt Jane was the first one to greet us. She came dashing out her front door and onto the front porch with her arms waving in the air. I just love her.

She and Mom opened their arms wide for a super big hug, and Mom requested John to get the baked beans, and me to get the chocolate cake. Aunt Jane gave me an awkward hug because the cake was in my way, and the next thing I knew, we both had chocolate frosting on our shirts.

She said, "Can I take that for you, Molly Jo?" And was I ever glad!

Claire came running out, calling my name. "Molly Jo, Molly Jo!" And she gave Grandma the biggest hug. I am so glad Grandma came with us.

Claire and I hugged each other for what seemed a minute. And Claire kept saying, "Nana, Nana, I missed you!" So funny that Claire calls Grandma "Nana" instead of "Grandma."

Grandma brought Claire a little box of presents from our trip: several postcards, a pen that writes in red or blue, some gummy candies, and a sparkly crystal glass ball that she can hang in her room to catch the light.

The only time I've ever seen Claire was when we lived in Nashville, and her family came to see us a few times. But now, it is simply crazy to say that we both live in Maine. Holy jelly beans.

John started asking Uncle Jim about his drone right away, hoping that he'd get to fly it while we were here. Aunt Jane said that Uncle Jim and Dad were in the woodshop, working on a large order of cabinets for a new house.

They are on a tight deadline, so the drone might have to wait until our next visit. Mom says maybe when we come back on the weekend. Uncle Jim's drone is super cool, and I would like to fly it too even though John says it's just for boys. Drones don't care if I am a boy or girl.

Aunt Jane led us down the winding brick path to the front door of the woodshop. Grace skipped with Smokey under her arm. Claire and I held hands and just jabbered away. John ran way ahead of us, and Mom locked arms with Grandma.

Uncle Jim's woodshop is so cute with a porch where Claire and I can play. The big wooden sign above the door says, "Daisy Designs" in wooden letters. We are the Daisy family, and this is where my Dad works.

Uncle Jim's woodshop is much bigger than the one Dad had in Tennessee. And it has more lights than I could believe! The ceiling is as bright as the open sky.

Uncle Jim said, "Hello!" in his big, cheerful voice when the door opened. And he chased Grace around the workshop while she giggled like she used to do in Tennessee.

Dad had a broad smile when he saw us come in. He and Uncle Jim were very dusty in their blue canvas aprons, but neither of them is the kind to fret over dirty clothes. The whole place smells so good, the sawdust and fresh paint and piles of neatly stacked wood.

Dad and Uncle Jim gave us a tour of their table saws and the sanders and all the chisels and clamps. I guess Grandpa Daisy liked to build things too, and some of his clamps and hammers were hung up next to his picture.

Grandma clapped her hands, and excitedly said, "Grandpa Daisy could never have enough clamps."

John asked Dad and Uncle Jim so many questions about the workshop. I didn't even realize he loved tools, but he begged Dad for a jigsaw for his birthday. Dad said, "Mom and I will keep that in mind, John! You really like tools, don't you?"

I asked, "What would you do with a jigsaw, John?"

"I might build something for your and Grace's room!" he said.

I didn't expect him to say that. He keeps surprising me with good brother deeds. I need to do something extra for him, but I keep forgetting.

I hadn't seen Dad this satisfied in a while. I could tell by the way he holds his coffee cup. It's hard to explain. Just something I know about my Dad. He holds his coffee cup higher when he's in a perfect mood.

Dad knows how to build cabinets like it's nobody's business. He's teaching Uncle Jim some of his fancy joint techniques like dovetails and butt joints (which makes me

laugh out loud). It's the only time I get to say butt and not get into trouble. Butt, butt, butt.

Suddenly, I heard Aunt Jane clearing her throat, and she spoke louder than her normal Aunt Jane's voice. "Attention, everybody. It's time for the workshop to close for the evening. It's dinner time!"

We all cheered!

Uncle Jim and Dad fired up the grill. Claire and I set the table with red and white napkins, paper plates, and silver spoons. John poured the beverages; we had a choice between lemonade and hot chocolate with marshmallows. Grace loaded a bowl with marshmallows for the hot chocolate. Mom helped Aunt Jane get out the catsup, mustard, the big dill pickles, and the baked beans. Grandma arranged a red glass plate with carrot sticks, little tomatoes, and cucumber slices.

The smell of those juicy burgers, hot dogs, and buttery corn was like heaven to me. I was so hungry I couldn't think straight. Finally, Dad and Uncle Jim came into the kitchen with a big platter of cheeseburgers and hot dogs. Nothing could have made this girl happier.

So thankful for my favorite foods ever: cheeseburgers, hot dogs, corn on the cob, carrot and cucumber sticks, Aunt Jane's homemade applesauce, and Mom's chocolate cake. After we finished eating, Mom said it was time to pack up and go. All of us kids said, "Aww!" at the same time. None of us wanted the fun to end, but it was a school night, and we still had to drive home and do our homework.

Grandma said, "But before we forget, we need to take a few pictures for Molly Jo's new photo frame." So, after a few pictures of all of us together, we helped clear the table and loaded the dishwasher. Then hugs and more hugs. Claire wanted to go home with us and spend the night; she kept pleading with Aunt Jane. But she wasn't allowed because it's a school night. I can't wait for her to visit us and to see Cherry Forest!

Grace and I piled into the van to go home with Mom and Grandma. John wanted to go back with Dad in the pickup truck.

As we backed out of Uncle Jim's driveway, Claire leaped up and down, waving goodbye with all her might and blowing kisses. I shook my arm out the window and hoped that Claire saw me. Grandma put her window down and blew kisses back to her. Grace put Smokey up to her window so Claire could see him.

A few seconds later, as we got onto the road, Mom started honking her horn and flashing her lights at Dad's pickup. Why is she doing that? What's the matter?

She said, "Look! Dad left his coffee mug on the roof of his truck, and he's driving around with it. It's going to topple off the truck."

Grandma, Grace, and I were holding our breath, hoping nothing terrible would happen. The coffee cup was still up there on his roof, barely holding on.

Mom honked her horn again and flashed her lights on and off over and over. Finally, Dad pulled over to the side of the road to figure out what was going on. Mom pulled over, too. When Dad got out of the car, he noticed Mom pointing at the roof of his truck and saw his mug.

He grabbed it and started drinking the coffee, just smiling. Mom and Grandma were just shaking their heads in disbelief.

At that moment, Grace and I started breathing again and then busted out laughing. Who drives around with a coffee cup on the roof of their truck? My Dad.

Wow, what a day. What an evening. We are still very new in Maine but visiting Aunt Jane's house reminded me of being home. I don't have a care in the world.

For the entire evening, I didn't even once think of Melissa or Chesterfield Lane. Not that I didn't want to, but I had such a good time at Aunt Jane's house that my head is filling up with brand new memories. That hasn't happened since we moved here.

I started remembering once again about the one thing that Grandma talked about. *Maybe I DO already have what I need.* All things considered; this was one of my best days in Maine so far.

Happiness Is Your Decision
Advice for a Remarkable Life

Many people search for happiness all their life. They hope someone will make them happy. They buy things to make them happy. If they don't find happiness, they might believe some people are lucky, and others are not.

But did you know that happiness is a decision? Yes, it's your decision. Every single day you can decide whether to be happy or not. You see, happiness comes from within.

So, you may wonder if it's that easy, why isn't everyone happy? It's quite simple. It's because people don't realize that happiness is an inside job! We must take ownership of it.

Happiness isn't something that we should wait on. Nope! Don't wait for sunny skies, your birthday, when you grow up or have more things. No, happiness isn't about those things.

It's about the blessings you already have, the thankfulness you have for your life, and how you look at things. Happiness is your decision, and you deserve to be happy every day of your life.

And the best part? If you're happy, you will spread it around.

CHAPTER 13:
THE ANNIVERSARY BOX

My Mom and Dad will have their 13th anniversary on Saturday. Every year, they follow the same tradition: they eat their anniversary dinner on a cardboard box. I am not making this up. I've heard them tell this story over and over.

When Mom and Dad got married, they lived in a small apartment inside a big red house at the corner of two main streets in Cheyenne, Wyoming. Their apartment was on the first floor of this big old house.

Mom says they would enter through the house's front door, and their apartment was on the left. Their living room overlooked their big front porch and East 19th Street. Their tiny apartment didn't even have a bedroom. I can't believe they didn't have a bedroom, but they had a bed, but not an ordinary bed.

My Dad says their bed was called a rollaway bed, a fold-down bed that has wheels. You can stand it up and roll it around the room. Not with people in it, but that would be so fun. They kept their rollaway bed standing up in a closet until it was time to go to bed. Then they rolled their mattress from the closet into the kitchen.

They pulled it down, unhooked the strap that held the mattress to the frame, and slept there, right in the kitchen. I can't imagine if my parents slept in our kitchen now.

In the morning, they did the whole process backward — smoothed the sheets and blankets, strapped the mattress to the frame, stood up the bed, rolled it into the closet, and shut the door. Strange? I think so.

I kind of wished Grace and I had a bed like that. During the day, we could have more room to play if our beds were in our closet.

Mom says they didn't have much to their names when they got married, so they got a furnished apartment, meaning it came with furniture. Mom says it was old furniture, but wonderfully comfortable.

On Mom and Dad's very first anniversary, they wanted to have a special dinner on a coffee table. But they didn't have a coffee table, so my Dad says he pulled out the big cardboard box that their Christmas tree came in. He laid the box on its side and sat it in front of the couch. Then Mom placed a towel with a diamond pattern over the box like a tablecloth. Mom added candles, flowers, plates, and napkins to their table. They had their anniversary dinner on that box: steak, baked potatoes, and salad.

My parents called this their "diamond top dinner," which sounds so fancy. They came up with that name because of the diamond pattern on the towel.

And they still have that same towel. Mom doesn't let us use the towel for baths or anything like that. She keeps it in the linen closet until it's their anniversary, and then she gets it out.

Every year since their first anniversary, they have had their "diamond top dinner" in the living room on their cardboard box covered by the same towel.

This Saturday is their 13th anniversary, and I bet that Dad will go up into the attic and get the box for their dinner and bring it down to the living room.

So, on Saturday morning – even before I got up – I could hear my Dad pulling down the squeaky ladder to the attic.

He rumbled around up there, moving things from one side of the attic to the other. I know he is searching for the box.

"Do you know where our box is?" he asked Mom in a muffled voice from the attic.

"What did you say?" she said from downstairs in a loud voice.

"Do you know where our box is?" Dad asked in an even louder but muffled voice.

"Well, we always kept it in the attic, but since we've moved, I've lost track of it," she yelled back, hoping Dad would hear her.

"Maybe it's in the garage or under our bed," she said in an even louder voice.

I could hear his heavy footsteps going back and forth up there. Then I heard him hurrying down the ladder, and I stayed in my bedroom, minding my own business.

I heard John announce from his bedroom, "Why don't you make an anniversary table for Mom from wood, Dad?"

Uh-oh. John doesn't get it.

"Because for the past 12 years, Mom and I have eaten our anniversary dinner on that same cardboard box, son. That's why. If we wanted a wooden table for our anniversary dinner, I would have made it years ago for your Mom."

"Oh," John said. And that's all he said because Dad is flustered and won't be happy until he finds their box.

I opened my bedroom door and peeked out, but quickly realized I didn't want to be involved in this hunt for the box.

Mom and Dad began checking all over the house for the box. Dad examined the garage, and Mom came upstairs to our rooms, inspecting under our beds and in our closets. Even Grandma started checking around, and so did us kids.

After about five minutes of searching the garage, I heard Dad say, "We should have been so careful about the box when we moved here. What were we thinking?"

"We were busy with so many things. We can find another box," Mom said with her shaky voice. It almost sounded like she would choke up.

A few minutes later, I heard Grandma clapping her hands and saying, "I found it. I found it."

"Where?" Dad asked.

"Yes, where?" Mom repeated.

"It's folded up and standing next to the washing machine," she said, beaming from ear to ear.

"Oh, my gosh, yes! Now I remember," Mom said, hiding her face with her hands. "I am the one who put the box there the day we arrived and had forgotten all about it."

"And we've been passing by it day in and day out," Dad said, looking astonished.

"It's all part of moving," said Grandma with a massive sigh of relief. "When things get shifted around and stored in different places, it's hard to keep track of where they are."

Grandma has moved more times than any of us because Grandpa Daisy was in the Air Force. If anybody knows, it would be her.

Dad says, "I'm glad we found the box, but even if we hadn't found it, we would have found a new box. It's the tradition that your Mom and I have that matters. The box can be replaced, and someday we will get a different one because this one is floppy and worn."

"Yeah, Dad, it is dilapidated," John said. "You and Mom should start searching for a new box soon. You can have the box my beanbag chair came in," he said eagerly, jumping and down like he did a lot.

"That's kind, John, but it's not the right shape to do the job, but I appreciate you thinking of that," Dad said.

We all felt better because Grandma found the box. She saved our whole family, and I just wanted to hug her.

I wasn't happy the anniversary box went missing, but the whole incident let me see my parents' real side. Even to THEM moving isn't all fun when things like this happen.

So tonight, Grandma will cook us kids a leisurely dinner. My parents will have their anniversary dinner later when we head upstairs.

When it got to be about 5:30, I heard Grandma wanting us to vote on what we want for dinner. Grace always says the same thing: peanut butter toast with scrambled eggs on top.

"Grace, we can't have that every day of the week. Didn't you just have it this morning?" Grandma asked.

"But I love it, Grandma, and I'll never, ever be tired of eggs and peanut butter toast."

"John, what would you like for dinner?" Grandma asked, a little less patiently this time.

"I'd like a cheese and pepperoni sandwich with pickles and a squirt of mustard and some olives on the side," John requested.

"You'll have some fruit and veggies on your plate, too, John," Grandma said.

"I'll have pea pods and a banana, Grandma."

"That sounds easy, John. Now, what about you, Molly Jo?"

"I'll have what you're having, Grandma."

"Okay, then it will be peanut butter toast and scrambled eggs."

I was okay with that.

John and I helped Grandma make dinner, and we ate it in the kitchen on paper plates. We helped Grandma clean up the kitchen, and then Mom and Dad came down to cook their anniversary dinner. Grandma said that all of us kids should scoot upstairs so that Mom and Dad could have some time together.

But I wanted to actually see the Diamond Top Dinner. Grandma broached the subject with Mom and Dad. They agreed that if we got our baths and into our pajamas without complaining, we could come down for a few minutes when their dinner was ready.

So, we took turns getting baths and pajamas on. Even John wanted to see the Anniversary Box with their dinner on top of it. After a little while, Grandma tapped on our bedroom doors and said we could go downstairs.

Grace went down first. She didn't really understand what it was all about, but she still tiptoed down the stairs, peeking through the spindles. For John and me, it felt like Christmas – that feeling you get when you sneak down the stairs and see the tree lit with a billion lights and all the presents underneath. We didn't know what to expect.

Mom wore a soft white dress, dangly crystal earrings, and high heels. They had music playing, the kind grownups like. Their cardboard box was all set up in the living room, covered by the diamond top towel.

Everything was so fancy – white china, cloth napkins, flowers on the table, and a lit candle. Mom and Dad invited us to sit at their table. John at Dad's spot and me at Mom's.

Each of them had an anniversary envelope on their plate for each other. And I spied a box of fancy chocolates, too. Dad knew right away that I wanted one.

He said, "Molly Jo, you can have one tomorrow. Each of you kids can enjoy a couple chocolates tomorrow," Dad said.

"It's time to go back upstairs, kids," Grandma said. "Let's reward your Mom and Dad with some time just for themselves."

I hoped they would invite us to stay down with them. I wanted to hear their stories, but I guess we are not allowed. Grandma tells us kids it's just one night, and it would not kill us to be upstairs.

So, upstairs we went. Grace and I snuggled up in Grandma's room. Grandma let Grace and me go into her card drawer and pull everything out.

She has six decks of cards, one rule book about card games, two foil-covered nature books (one about trees and one about birds), a little magnifying glass, a package of new dice, napkins with red bicycles printed on them and a white hanky that belonged to Grandpa Daisy.

Grandma is teaching Grace and me how to play solitaire, but Grace doesn't understand why you play solitaire alone.

I love going into Grandma's room because it's packed with treasures. She has a row of clear bottles half-filled with colored water that sparkles in the sunlight on her window ledge.

While Grace and I were in Grandma's room, John examined his bug collection through his microscope. Can you believe he brought dead bugs from our yard on Chesterfield Lane all the way to Maine? Dad says it was all right because John had preserved them with that smelly liquid.

My parents had their 13th diamond top anniversary dinner. Even Dad and Grace are playing sock ball again when he comes home from work.

It's good that certain things don't change even when you move. But then... some things do, which means that next week I must do my presentation about Nashville at my new school. My stomach hurts thinking about it. But I am glad I won't be alone because Anna Lin, the other new girl, will be there with me.

Everything Is Difficult Before It Is Easy
Advice for a Remarkable Life

The first time you try something, it may seem hard until you get the hang of it. Think of tying your shoes and how many times you had to do that before you could tie your shoes well! Everyone goes through learning curves. Some things will come easy to you and other things hard. You must give your brain a chance to learn it.

When you are learning to swim, initially it can seem scary and almost impossible. But once it clicks and you figure it out, it's hard to even remember what it was like before you knew how to swim.

The same thing goes for riding a bicycle. The first time you got on a bike, you may have wondered how in the world you can keep your bike from falling over. But you practice, and then you practice some more, and before you know it, you can ride around with ease.

It's that way with almost anything you learn! Multiplication, cooking, drawing, playing a musical instrument, learning to speak in a different language. First, it is awkward, then becomes more comfortable with practice.

Don't worry that some people learn faster. Faster isn't always better (as you probably know from the tortoise and the hare). What is easy for you might be difficult for someone else. Every time you start something new, remember that learning takes time and patience.

CHAPTER 14:
THE CLASS PRESENTATION

The day arrived for Anna Lin and me to tell our classmates about the towns where we used to live. I felt butterflies in my stomach, but Grandma told me this morning to think of it as easy and fun.

Dad gave me a brain trick idea to try today. He told me, "One way to feel confident is to make yourself big rather than small when getting up in front of your class."

Dad knows it's not easy for me to go in front of people. I guess I mumble and cross my arms usually.

He said, "So when you go to the front for your presentation, speak up and open your arms as if you are welcoming someone new to the classroom. You'll be surprised how much more confident you'll feel!"

Really? Maybe it's another one of those things I don't have to understand for it to work. I will try it.

Ms. Jewel said a big hello to Anna Lin and me when we got to school. Her face blossomed into a big smile. She told us we'd do our presentation the first thing and not to stress. Her words settled down my butterflies and Anna Lin's too.

After Mr. Dasher, our principal, made the school announcements, Ms. Jewel told the class today was truly special. Why? Because Anna Lin and I will do our presentation about the places where we used to live.

Ms. Jewel invited Anna Lin and me to take seats at the front table in our classroom. We wrote our notes on the easel board. She said we could start by telling one thing about where we lived. I cleared my throat, pushed back my hair, and said, "I used to live in Nashville, the capital of Tennessee."

I could not believe I said that. My mind was running 100 miles per hour. I wanted to say something far more interesting, but it was the first thing that fell out of my mouth. Ack! Boring!

So, Kyla, my classmate, said, "Does that mean there is a fancy capitol building in downtown Nashville, Molly Jo?"

"Yes, Kyla. Our class went there on a field trip one October day and had our pictures taken on the steps of the capitol building. And afterward, we got to stop by the Peanut Shop."

Then the class wondered what the Peanut Shop was. I said, "It's my favorite candy shop in all the world!"

They wondered why it was named the Peanut Shop. I said, "Because they have peanuts! But they also have gummies, sour candy, malted milk balls, chocolate covered pretzels, chocolate raisins, chocolate almonds and boiled peanuts and …"

Then Ms. Jewel said, "Thank you, Molly Jo. Now it's Anna Lin's turn to tell one thing."

Anna Lin stood up, paused, and didn't say a word.

Ms. Jewel said, "Anna Lin, now it's your turn. Would you tell the class what town you used to live in and one thing about it?"

I worried for her; her teeth were chattering, and she wasn't saying a word. Nothing. Then out of the silence, she blurted out, "I used to live in Caribou, Maine."

Ms. Jewel asked the class if anyone had ever been there, and two kids shouted, "Yes!"

Ms. Jewel asked Anna Lin if she'd tell the class the best thing about living in Caribou.

Anna Lin took a big breath and rattled off a list of things she loved from Caribou. "I love going to the winter festival in February! We go snow skiing and ice skating and play broomball, build snowmen and go sledding on cardboard sleds and drink hot chocolate and roast marshmallows…"

Ms. Jewel said, "Class, doesn't that sound like a fun place to live?"

Seemed like everyone wanted to live in Caribou.

Then Ms. Jewel asked me to tell the class how living in Tennessee was different than living here in Maine.

"Oh, the weather is much different! It is warmer in Tennessee, and we don't get much snow as you get here. In Tennessee, we must drive a long way to see the ocean, but here it's not far away. And in Tennessee, we have Meat and Three's."

Ms. Jewel said, "Molly Jo, can you tell the class what you mean by Meat and Three?"

"Okay, it's when you go to a restaurant and choose the meat you want, like fried chicken, meatloaf, or country ham, and then you pick three sides."

"Oh!" said Ms. Jewel. I get it. "Class, do you get it, too? It sounds so good, doesn't it? You get to choose whatever meat you want, and then you get to choose three other sides to go with it like creamed corn, mashed potatoes, or peas."

"Except I don't like peas, Ms. Jewel. But I do love macaroni and cheese."

Then Ms. Jewel added, "And if you don't like meat, you could just have sides!"

Suddenly, Anna Lin and I were like the stars in our class. The kids were talking about the Peanut Shop and the Winter Festival, and it became fun. I never in my long life expected to have fun speaking in front of my class!

We learned that Ms. Jewel once lived in Caribou, so that made Anna Lin's eyes sparkle like I've never seen. Now she and Ms. Jewel have fun stuff to talk about together.

And some of the kids in my class have visited Nashville. I thought my heart would do a fun flip flop! One girl, Maggie, has an Uncle Paul who lives there. Another classmate used to live in California, which is much further away than Tennessee. And she seems happy living here, so who knows?

Ms. Jewel told Anna Lin and me that we could retake our seats. I couldn't believe I enjoyed being in front of the class. Then Charlotte and Jeffrey, probably the friendliest kids in my class, told Anna Lin and me, and the whole class, about living in Maple River.

Charlotte knows that I like to write and do calligraphy, and she told us about a store downtown where young writers meet on Saturdays. She said, "The Writers of Maple River meet on the Square, and they welcome all ages."

I didn't know that I could meet with other writers! I wonder what they do when they meet.

Ms. Jewel said, "You can share your compositions with the other writers and learn from them. How exciting!"

Charlotte also said, "The hobby shop on Chapman Street has rocks, crystals, and drone supplies. They may even have fancy pens and markers. Oh, and paper and pencils for drawing, too.

"And on the first Saturday of the month, ask your parents to take you to the Maple River Fire Department because you might get to take a tour of the fire engine.

"Another favorite thing my family likes to do is to go to the seaside town of Boothbay. We go to the Festival of Lights in December. Once you go there, you will be hooked and want to go back every single year.

"They have horse-drawn carriage rides and boats decorated in twinkly lights in the harbor. And Maple River has a Christmas parade that will melt your heart. If your family decides to go, we can give you hints on where the best places are to watch it. Go early and get hot cocoa with marshmallows."

Drawing by Henry Morris

Jeffrey got up and rushed to the front of the class. He said, "Anna Lin and Molly Jo, tell your parents about the Maple River Ice Cream Shop. It's right downtown on the square.

Drawing by
Ashlyn Lindow

"If you've never had real blueberry ice cream here in Maine, then you're in for a treat because theirs is the best in the world. My brothers like their Monster shakes, and my whole family loves their Salted Caramel sundaes.

"But don't go on Saturday afternoons. You'll be waiting on the sidewalk for at least an hour.

"And in November, my grandparents get cabins for our whole family, even my cousins, and we come together to celebrate Thanksgiving. We roast marshmallows around a campfire and build teepees. In the afternoons, we play kickball – the kids against the adults and sometimes we have a rock, paper scissors contest.

"We like to go on the lake with my Grandpa's canoe and go fishing from the dock. That is, if it's not too cold and many years it definitely is! We make the best family memories there.

"One last thing. We like to go to Christmas Cove in the summer to watch the sailboats and pleasure crafters. It's a feast for your eyes!"

I can't wait to tell Mom and Dad about this stuff. I wish we could do these things right now! Maybe we could invite Melissa's family for Thanksgiving at the cabins.

Suddenly, living in Maine isn't as strange as when I arrived. I thought Maine was far from everything I know but realizing that some kids have visited Nashville helps.

I can't wait to tell Grandma how it went for me today; I grumbled about it way too much, but I think I passed with flying colors. At first, being in front of the class seemed hard, but then it got easier. I must thank Ms. Jewel for that. Inside my head, I did a little victory dance.

It's for real, an actual official fact that I would like to be a speaker when I grow up, even though this is the very first time I've ever thought about this in my whole life.

CHAPTER 15:
THE PIANO THAT DISAPPEARED

When we lived in TN, we had a piano, a lovely piano. But we couldn't bring it with us to Maine. Dad says it costs too much to move it. That made me sad even though I didn't play the piano, but Mom does.

Dad gave the piano to Mom as a surprise one Christmas Eve a long time ago. I was super young, but I can still remember her excitement. She was in the kitchen, washing dishes, and looking out the window when the music truck drove up to our driveway. She ran all around the house, not knowing what to do.

That Christmas was the best, and the first time I remember us singing Christmas carols around the piano. And then we'd play and sing year-round.

Mom's face glowed when she played the piano. She taught us certain songs that were fun to sing together like "Carolina Moon" and "A Fox Went Out on a Chilly Night." And, of course, we learned many Christmas songs, too. I can still remember us kids singing those songs while Mom played piano, and Dad played the autoharp.

At Christmas, we would invite our friends and neighbors to our house for a caroling party. It was more than a caroling party because everyone brought food and snacks to share. Our house would be all decorated with lights inside.

We had games for the little kids like "pin the tail on Rudolph" and prizes for the winners. At the end of the party, before everyone went home, Mom played Christmas carols, and all of us would gather around the piano and sing and play bells. Even Melissa's dog, Freckles, loved to listen to our caroling.

But now I realize we won't be having caroling parties because we don't have a piano, and we don't even know anyone to invite. I doubt it will feel like Christmas without our piano.

One day back in Tennessee, right before we moved, our piano just disappeared, and my parents didn't mention it. I didn't want to ask Mom because I knew she would be sad. I just didn't know what to do about it.

Maybe my secret book will help me figure out how to get a new piano for Mom.

I really hoped that I could have my own room at our new house, but since that is not going to happen, maybe we can save money for a new piano for Mom. That night when Dad got home from the workshop, I told him I needed to talk privately with him.

I pulled out the $32.67 from my pocket that I had saved to buy art supplies and ice cream. I told Dad I would donate it to get Mom a new piano.

His face lit up, and he said, "Molly Jo, that is the kindest thought ever. It will surely cost more than $32.67 to get a new piano for Mom, but I will keep this safe. I know this is a lot of money for you to set aside for Mom's piano."

I saved money for months to get $32.67, but Grandma believes what I give away will come back to me if I have good reasons in my heart. I hope that my Mom can get a piano again, but it seems like it will take forever to save up enough money.

Best Way to Compare
Advice for a Remarkable Life

Do you sometimes compare yourself to other people? Do you know what comparing does? It usually leaves you feeling sad. Yes, sad because you may feel like you don't measure up to someone else.

What would it be like if there were a much better way to compare? Let's say you're trying to become better at drawing or playing the piano. (And if you don't do either, just play along with me for a minute.)

Instead of judging yourself compared to other people, why not compare yourself to the person you were a year ago?

Have your skills improved? Can you draw better or play better than last year this time? Have you been practicing? If you're dragging along and not seeing improvement or making strides, figure out what you need to do to advance yourself. Almost always, the answer is more and better practice sessions.

That kind of comparing is excellent because you're working on the best version of yourself. If you're not happy with where you are, you have the magical powers to improve if you practice and stay the course.

Remember, most people don't suddenly become great at something. They practice and put in many hours when nobody is watching. Learn to appreciate yourself and keep striving to do better. Be proud of your progress.

Let others inspire you but not make you sad. And don't ever forget to notice how far you have come.

CHAPTER 16:
DINNER WITH THE NEIGHBORS

I really miss our neighbors from Tennessee, especially Melissa's family. Melissa's Mom would invite us for dinner, and sometimes it would be on the spur of the moment. I loved it when that happened, especially when Mom was going to serve something I didn't enjoy like stewed tomatoes.

Sometimes Melissa's Mom would make her famous homemade lasagna and bread. She would always serve a yummy tossed green salad in a giant blue bowl with tomatoes, cucumbers, and feta cheese.

Melissa's house had a giant rectangular table big enough for both our families. It had long wooden benches, which are much more fun than ordinary chairs. I always sat at the end because if you sat in the middle, it was hard to get out without kicking the person beside you.

I loved those times. If it was a weekend night, Melissa invited me for a sleep-over, or I asked her. I preferred going to Melissa's house because she had her own room, but she enjoyed coming to our house because she liked to play with Grace. Melissa loved the desk that we nudged up to the window. We'd gaze out the window for hours.

But here, here in Maple River, we don't know our neighbors as we did in Nashville. Everybody in the neighborhood seems to know each other except us. Grandma thinks that's just part of being new – we must give it time to become a part of the community.

Today just might be the beginning because one of our neighbors, who lives right across the street in the house with the yellow glass door, dropped over unexpectedly. She even brought us an amazing homemade blueberry pie. When I first saw her standing on our front porch, I couldn't take my eyes off the hair on top of her head. It almost looked like a bird's nest.

She introduced herself to Mom and said, "Hi there, and welcome to our neighborhood. My name is Darla Simmons. And my husband's name is Chuck Simmons, but he's not with me. He's at work." Then she handed that beautiful pie to Mom, who gasped with admiration and winced when she felt how heavy it was. Must be hundreds of blueberries in it.

Mom said, "Oh, my goodness, what a beautiful pie! Nice to meet you, Darla! Won't you please come in?"

Ms. Darla said, "Yes, I'd love to but for just a few minutes. I'm waiting for the plumber to repair our toilet. The water rose up and spilled onto the floor almost to the hallway."

And then she cupped her hand over her mouth to whisper something to Mom. It sounded like, "The smell! The rugs will never be the same."

Mom just said, "Eww!"

Ms. Darla quickly responded by saying, "No worries. The rugs have been washed and sanitized, and I've bleached the floor. Nothing but fresh, clean smell now."

And along with Ms. Darla was a young boy that she introduced as Stephen, their grandson. He's just a little older than Grace and taller than her.

Ms. Darla said, "Chuck and I are so excited to have a new family in this house!"

Mom said, "Well, we're delighted to be here for sure!"

Delighted? That is not the word I would choose, but Mom likes to be extra nice.

Ms. Darla said that her husband worked at the hobby store downtown. Hearing where he worked, my ears nearly flew around my head. Could it be the same hobby store that Charlotte told us about at school?

I kept admiring the juicy homemade blueberry pie Ms. Darla brought over. The crust on the top of the pie was woven together like a basket and shone with sparkled sugar. I wondered if we will be allowed to have a piece after Ms. Darla goes home. I love blueberries, and it's a miracle to live in Maine, where blueberries are everywhere.

Before Ms. Darla left, she invited our family to come for dinner tomorrow evening. And Mom said, "Absolutely, yes! Y'all are so kind! What can we bring?"

Ms. Darla said, "Just bring yourselves, and I like your southern accent."

Oh gosh! We hardly know them, and do we have to stay all the way through dinner and come up with things to say? I sure hope their toilet works by then. No way am I going in their bathroom where it spilled onto the floor and soaked the rugs. That would be a scary situation even if Ms. Darla has shampooed the carpets.

Mom said, "Thank you for coming over, Darla, and for introducing us to Stephen! And that pie! My husband is going to do backflips when he sees it. You have no idea how much he loves berry pies! He would eat pie every day of the week if I made it."

And I wanted to say I would too, but I kept silent.

Ms. Darla and Stephen left, and I was full of questions.

"Can we have some of that pie now, Mom? And I wished you baked pies every day because I'm like Dad and I would eat pie every day. And do we all have to go to dinner tomorrow night?"

Mom said, "Whoa, Molly Jo. First, let's wait for Dad. We'll have pie for dessert tonight. And second, if I baked pies every day, they wouldn't be so special. And third, you bet we're all going for dinner to the Simmons house. That was especially kind of them to ask us. It's a family event, and I accepted on behalf of all of us, so we'll be there. Molly Jo, it will be fun!"

Nobody asks us kids about these things. Are we invisible or something?

John overheard the conversation and said, "I'll go, Mom. It will be cool to meet them."

The next evening at six, it was time to go to the Simmons house for dinner. Everybody except me seemed okay with it. Grace wanted to play with Stephen, and Mom looks forward to making friends with neighbors. She told John that he could ask Mr. Simmons about the Hobby Shop.

His jaw dropped, and he said, "A person can do that?"

"Of course, John," Mom said. "I bet he would be flattered for you to ask him some questions."

Even though Ms. Darla told my Mom she didn't need to bring a thing to dinner, Mom said, "It doesn't matter – you still take something." So, she made two loaves of homemade bread that filled our house with a heavenly aroma: one loaf to take and one to keep here.

Grandma stayed home for the evening. I figured she might because she had on her bunny slippers and wanted some peaceful time for reading. She says there's nothing as blissful as silence for a little while.

Couldn't I stay home with Grandma? Pretty please?

Mom spoke to all of us kids before we left, but I am positive she was only talking to me. She said, "Please address Chuck and Darla as Mr. and Mrs. Simmons. In Nashville, we would call them Mr. Chuck and Ms. Darla, but here, they use last names. And it's the proper thing to do."

We all agreed, even though it doesn't sound as friendly to say Mr. and Mrs. It seems stuffy!

When we got to their house, which is right across the street from ours, John rang the doorbell. Their bright yellow front door with shiny glass smelled like fresh paint, and their house number was in fancy tiles above their door.

Upon ringing the doorbell, I could feel the vibrations of people rushing to the front door. The door opened wide, and there was a giant man, whom I suppose is Mr. Simmons, with his tall, clumsy dog.

Mr. Simmons wore a light blue long-sleeved shirt with yellow plaid pants, and suspenders to hold up his pants. I have not seen my Dad wear anything like that, but Mr. Simmons seems proud of his attire.

Mr. Simmons, who has curly blond hair and glasses, is mighty tall – nearly as big as the door. As he stood there at the door, he said, "Welcome, Daisy family! Please come in," with a very loud, but friendly voice.

All five of us walked in amidst the loud chatter inside the front door. The Simmons' big scruffy dog put his paws on me – not on my knees, but on my shoulders. And his big wet nose nearly touched my lips! Ack! I backed up, and my heart was pumping like a speeding train.

Mr. Simmons sort of apologized, but not as much as I hoped he would. Who lets their giant dog put their hairy paws on a kid's shoulders like that? I mean, me, the new neighbor girl.

Mr. Simmons said, "His name is Buffalo, and he adores attention. Don't let his playfulness bother you. Most of the time he is sleeping on the recliner over there. The old boy is ten years old and lazy as a napping sloth."

I let out a big sigh of relief when Buffalo lost interest in me and went back to his chair.

While the parents were loudly chatting in the hallway, my eyes popped out like a robot in admiration of their lovely home. Their living room is luxurious with a blue velvet couch in the shape of an "L" and a long silver coffee table with an enormous bowl of golden fruit. A giant painting of an elephant mama with her babies hangs on the long wall above the couch. Oh, how I admire it!

Standing next to a pillar in the living room, I saw a tall wooden giraffe that I could barely take my eyes off. The giraffe is at least six or seven feet tall. I wondered where in the world they ever got it. I cannot imagine my parents having anything this full of awesomeness in our house. I wished that Grandma had come with us because she would simply flip cartwheels if she saw their giraffe.

The Simmons house is as pleasant as a furniture store where everything goes perfectly well together. Nothing catawampus in view. And their home is as spic and span as any home I've ever imagined, with nothing out of place. Even the shoes at the front door are lined up in a row from small to large.

Oh, how I wished our house could be like this! Everything so fancy and shiny and matchy-matchy. But I know that comparing my house to the Simmons' house isn't a good idea even though I love their place. Their giraffe is the best!

Mrs. Simmons said that dinner is nearly ready and that we can lounge in the living room until it is served. Mom wondered how she could help, and soon they were both in the kitchen talking up a storm.

Mr. Simmons makes funny, grunting noises that you can hear if you stand next to him. And his chest whistles when he breathes, but he is a genuinely nice man even though his nose hair is curly.

He marched us downstairs to see their magnificent fish tank. Their aquarium, which is about six feet long, lights up like an underwater city with peachy pink sand, rocks of many sizes, and the most beautiful shells I've seen. I even spied a golden treasure chest with a beautiful green bottle lying on its side.

Mr. Simmons allowed John to feed the fish a tiny sprinkle of food. As soon as John stretched his arm above the aquarium, the fish started swimming up, hoping to be the first ones to eat. He dropped the flakes a little at a time, and the family of fish raced to the top. Grace kept giggling and saying, "Do it again, John."

John told Dad, "I wish we could have an aquarium just like this at home. I would help care for it. I promise!"

And Mr. Simmons says, "Best hobby you could have, John. I'd be glad to give you and your Dad some tips."

Dad tapped the side of his cheek with his finger and said, "We'll see, John. We'll see. We have lots of settling in to do first."

We headed back upstairs because Mrs. Simmons said that dinner was ready. I never expected this, but they were having homemade pizza! It wasn't even a Friday night. I figured we may have had meatloaf or chicken legs and peas. But no, it was one of my favorite things, pizza! Does your family ever get to have pizza on a weeknight?

Mrs. Simmons made three kinds: cheese, pepperoni, and one with ham and pineapple, my favorite in the world. Mrs. Simmons said they usually don't make ham and pineapple pizza because Stephen is allergic to pineapple. Still, since we are guests, she thought we might like it.

Eating dinner at the Simmons in their fancy dining room is very deluxe. Instead of paper plates, they use china plates, like the kind when you're having mashed potatoes and roast beef. Mrs. Simmons gave us each a cloth napkin, and it wasn't lemonade that he poured in our glasses. He poured a sparkly, bubbly strawberry drink that Mrs. Simmons says they have when they celebrate something. Celebrate? What could they be celebrating? Mrs. Simmons clanged on her glass with her fork, and everyone glanced her way.

She spoke in a louder-than-normal voice and said, "We are happy to have the Daisy family as our new neighbors. We officially want to welcome you to our neighborhood."

Then Mr. Simmons also clanged on his glass with his fork, and in his big, deep chuckling voice, he said, "I second what she said. Welcome to Maple River, all you Daisys. We're glad you're here." We tapped our cups against each other's as if being here made us all excited.

Mr. Simmons laughs a deep-down-belly-laugh every time he says our last name, Daisy. Mom and Dad spoke up, saying how happy we are to be here and that we all appreciate their warm welcome.

Then Mrs. Simmons said it was time to "dig in" and start passing the pizza. I took three pieces of ham and pineapple pizza because I was super hungry and because it's my favorite kind in the world. Dad kind of gave me "the look" like I should have only taken two slices. Oops, I took three, and it's not polite to put them back. I'd be in more trouble if I did that.

The Simmons family passed honey around the table. Who eats honey with their pizza? Well, I found out it was a tradition for their family to dip their pizza crust into honey. You know, the leftover crust after you eat the part with the sauce and toppings.

My family has a pizza tradition too. It's not honey, but pickles. We like to have pickles with our pizza. Doesn't matter if they are dill or sweet pickles. Or sometimes olives. I wanted to speak up and tell the Simmons about pickles and pizza, but I waited too long. They were already onto something else.

Mrs. Simmons was excited for us to try the pizza because she made the sauce herself. She said she added fennel to it from their backyard garden.

"What's fennel?" I blurted out without thinking.

"It's an herb from our garden, Molly Jo, and it's perfect for pizza sauce," said Mrs. Simmons.

"Oh, ok."

Then I tasted the pizza, and nothing in the world would have prepared me for this taste in my mouth.

I didn't like that fennel. Not at all. It was a disgusting flavor that you should not have in pizza. I tried not to show how much I disliked it, but I am sure Mrs. Simmons noticed because she waited for me to tell her I loved it.

I didn't want to swallow and have that fennel go down my throat. I wanted to say "yum," but that was i-m-p-o-s-s-i-b-l-e. More than impossible. I held my breath so I wouldn't smell it and reached for my fizzy strawberry drink, hoping I could wash the pizza down. I ran my tongue over my lips, hoping to catch any extra drips of berry flavor. Still, I gagged a little but told Mrs. Simmons it was incredibly delicious. I wasn't lying because the strawberry drink was very yummy. So good, I drank the whole glass.

Mrs. Simmons said, "Molly Jo, there's plenty of pizza, and you can help yourself to more when you are ready."

I couldn't look in her eyes, but I quietly said, "Okay, sure, Mrs. Simmons. Thanks!"

I would never say this out loud, but I will never be ready to have more of that terrible fennel pizza.

I dipped a bit of my pizza crust into the pool of honey I had on my plate. That sweet sugary taste helped me get over the yucky fennel flavor.

John began asking all kinds of questions about the hobby store, and that put the spotlight onto him. Whew! I took the opportunity to wrap my pizza pieces inside my napkin, which then fell onto the floor. Buffalo noticed immediately. He crouched under my chair and started gobbling the pizza and the napkin as if he hadn't eaten all day. Keep chowing down until all that pizza disappears, I said to Buffalo in my head. And he did. And then he wanted more.

John said, "Mr. Simmons, I heard you work at the hobby store downtown."

"Work there? I own it, John! That's our family store, and Darla is there on Tuesdays and Thursdays. She does all the ordering. Me? I'm there most of the time. I do just about everything else. You're welcome to stop by anytime. We have merchandise everyone in your family will enjoy. Even your Grandma."

My ears perked up when Mr. Simmons said they owned the hobby store. I could hardly believe it. The Simmons family must be famous in Maple River.

John said, "I heard you have rock collections and maybe even bug collections. That's what I like."

Mr. Simmons said, "I can do you one better than that, John. You can meet other rock hounds at our store. They meet monthly and bring in their collections. We have a store calendar that lets you know when they meet. In fact, you can swap rocks with them, if you wish."

I could see John's eyes grow as large as quarters. This was like heaven to him.

Grace shook her head repeatedly and said that she didn't like rocks or bugs. Only stickers and teddy bears.

Mr. Simmons said they didn't have teddy bears, but they have all kinds of stickers that Grace would like. Grace swung her feet back and forth and nodded with a smile.

Dad told Mr. Simmons that I liked calligraphy, and Mr. Simmons chuckled loudly, with a huge belly laugh. He said, "Darla likes to do calligraphy, and because of her, we have a section in the store with writing pens, markers, fancy papers and books from which to learn. Molly Jo will have a heyday there."

I wonder when we'll get to go there! I hope Grandma takes us because she's never hurried. Sometimes Mom is in a big rush because she has a long to-do list and other errands like grocery shopping, but Grandma usually does just one thing at a time.

The most interesting part about having dinner at the Simmons was when they told us about the family who used to live in our house, the Silver family. I never even thought about the people that used to live in our house. Does that mean something is wrong with me? Did their Dad get a new job like my Dad? Or did they just want a different house? Or something else.

Mrs. Simmons says the people who used to live in our house were a family of five like ours – except they had three boys. I wanted to tell her we are a family of six counting Grandma. I wished that someone had spoken up, like Mom or Dad. Just because Grandma didn't come to dinner doesn't mean that she doesn't count.

Mrs. Simmons said that the family's youngest boy was a little older than me, and his name is Christopher. Mrs. Simmons said that Christopher stayed in the same room as Grace and me. His next older brother shared the room with him. So, it was a boys' room before now. Eww. Smelly socks and bugs and dirty clothes on the floor. Boy germs.

Mr. Simmons said it was hard for the Silver family to leave Maple River because the boys loved Cherry Forest. He said we'd probably find remnants of things they built in the woods like cool stick forts and rope swings. And Mrs. Simmons said, "Don't forget, Chuck, the bat houses and insect shelters they made too. And the boys always paraded around with their walking sticks."

Mr. Simmons became solemn and spoke directly to us kids in a surprisingly soft voice. "Kids, never take Cherry Forest for granted. It's the home of many woodland animals. The trees are a splendor in the winter when they are dusted with snow, and you will find yourselves making memories that most kids only dream about."

Dad said, "Amen, Chuck. It's one of the reasons we love this place."

I never realized how much people like Cherry Forest, but even Grandma is smitten with it. Mr. Simmons got up from his chair and excused himself. Mrs. Simmons said she knew what he was about to do. Shortly Mr. Simmons came back with a piece of paper that was rolled up and tied with a ribbon.

He said, "Daisy family, I've been entrusted with this map of Cherry Forest that has been handed down from family to family who've lived in your house. And now it's yours. The map has been updated several times, so it's current. Take note that a future ninja course was in the plans by the Silver family who recently moved.

"Their children really wanted a ninja course, but their move pre-empted that. So, who knows? Maybe it will be your desire to build a ninja course. Darla and I wish we had Cherry Forest in our backyard."

We all poured over the map, especially John. I had no idea Cherry Forest was such a mystical place. Maybe Dad can build a little cabin back there for us.

We didn't have dessert at the Simmons. They passed the honey around again so we could dip our pizza crust into it. And the parents had coffee. I left the table at the very first chance I got. Stephen wondered if I wanted to go back downstairs to see the fish tank again, and I said yes! I took Grace with me too. No little girl likes fennel; I'm sure of that.

John stayed at the table, glued to his seat, while Mr. Simmons told stories about Cherry Forest and places where he'd found amazing rocks. I was happy to escape the yucky pizza. I've never said those two words in a sentence before, but this pizza was yucky, I'm sorry to say.

As we left the Simmons house, Mr. Simmons gave the coveted map to Dad and said, "Bought any snow shovels yet?"

John said, "Can we get one, Dad? We'll get to stay home from school often, and I can help you."

Mr. Simmons chuckled. "John, you might have enjoyed snow days in Nashville, but here in Maple River, seldom do they close schools for snow. The snowplows will be out in full force here. You'll see, it will be fun."

Oh, there goes the snow days I dreamed about. I thought we'd have more snow days in Maine. I mean, it snows here much more than Nashville. This isn't fair at all.

Mrs. Simmons said, "There's plenty of time to think about snow. Autumn is just getting started. Let's not rush things for the Daisy family."

Mom gave a big sigh. Dad did too.

Mrs. Simmons said, "Oh, don't leave yet. I just remembered I have something for you."

Then she scurried to the kitchen, and we could hear her opening the cupboard doors. She came out with a jar of some green-ish stuff and two cans.

"Fresh fennel from the garden!" she said. "This is what I wanted to share with you. Fennel is great in pizza sauce and wonderful in meatballs too. And here are two cans of brown bread for your family. Slice it up and serve it warm with a pat of butter or cream cheese. You'll be in heaven and wanting more."

Mom gave Mrs. Simmons a hug and said she couldn't wait to try these at home.

I wondered why anybody would keep bread in a can. Didn't Mom consider this highly unusual?

When we got home that night, Grandma was in her blue-flowered flannel nightgown. She gave a jaw-gaping yawn and said that she was headed to her room to sip on her orange spice tea and read more pages of her book. I wanted more than anything to tell her about the hobby store and the giraffe – and the bread in a can – but Dad says I need to wait until tomorrow. Waiting is so hard. I can't stand waiting.

When I got home from school the next day, Grandma was relaxed in her easy chair with her hands folded in her lap, and I knew that she had time to listen to me.

I told her about that tall wooden giraffe in the Simmons' living room, and her eyes brightened.

"I wished we could have a giraffe at our house instead of just ordinary stuff like lamps and tables. Do you have any idea where they would get a wooden giraffe, Grandma?"

"Well, no, Molly Jo, I wasn't there. Did you ask Mr. or Mrs. Simmons about that?"

"No, Grandma, that didn't cross my mind."

"Molly Jo, it would have been ok to ask them. Being curious about their giraffe would probably have made them enormously proud! Maybe it's something that has been in their family for ages. Or maybe, they went on a safari and got it," she said as she hugged herself with glee!

I replied, "Mrs. Simmons says you can come over and see it anytime you want."

Grandma giggled about that and clapped with glee; she loves jungle animals.

Grandma and Grandpa Daisy used to collect miniature jungle animals and display them in a wooden cabinet with glass doors and lights that turned on at night. I loved peeking in that cabinet and dreaming of getting to keep those adorable dainty animals one day.

After Grandpa Daisy died, Grandma always kept the jungle animal collection in that cabinet. But Grandma left the wooden cabinet in Tennessee and only brought the animals with her.

She keeps the miniature jungle animals in a big round silver tin that cookies used to come in. Sometimes she lets me open the tin to pick out an animal, and then Grandma tells me stories about where it came from.

Some of them came from crackerjack boxes when Grandma and Grandpa were kids.

Oh! I almost forgot to tell Grandma about the Simmons' hobby store, and I gasped because she will not believe what I'm about to say to her.

"Grandma, do you remember when Anna Lin and I did our presentation at class about where we used to live?"

"Well, of course, Molly Jo. How could I forget about that?"

"Do you remember that Charlotte told us about a hobby store that John would like?"

"Yes, I remember something about that," she said, scratching her head a little.

"Well, Grandma, that hobby store belongs to the Simmons."

"The Simmons? You mean the people across the street?"

"Yes, our neighbors. They own it. I just can't believe it. It's the same store that Charlotte talked about."

"Well, dear, it's a small world. This isn't the first time that you will be amazed like that. I bet John will enjoy going there."

"John? Yes, and me too, Grandma."

"Well then, you can both go with me sometime soon."

"Okay! Maybe we can go today then."

"And maybe we can wait for a few days, Molly Jo," Grandma said. "There's plenty of time for everything. Don't worry, the hobby store isn't going anywhere, I promise."

"Grandma, did you know that some people add fennel to their pizza sauce? Mrs. Simmons does."

"Fennel on pizza?"

"Yes, that's what Mrs. Simmons calls it. She says it comes from their garden."

"Well, lucky for me, I stayed home last night, Molly Jo. I'm not a fan of fennel, even though Grandpa loved it. He liked it in his meatballs."

"Yuck!"

"Yes, I feel the same, Molly Jo. Double triple yuck."

"Mrs. Simmons gave some fennel to Mom to use. What can we do about that?"

Grandma winked at me and said, "No worries, Molly Jo. I'll find the fennel and put it in a very safe place."

My tricky Grandma. She and I are like two peas in a pod.

"And what about those cans of bread, Grandma? We're not going to really eat those, are we?"

"You might like brown bread, Molly Jo. It's slightly sweet."

"You've had it before, Grandma?"

"Yes, we had it growing up, Molly Jo. My sister, your great Aunt Peach, loved brown bread for breakfast, warmed up with a pat of butter on it. Oh, such good memories. Just try it when Mom serves it. It's something people here in New England enjoy, and you may find it's quite special too."

My ears were so shocked that they nearly fell to my lap when Grandma told me she has heard of bread in a can.

Be Grateful for the Little Things
Advice for a Remarkable Life

Make it a point to be thankful for the everyday things in your life like your pillow, a good night's rest, your toothbrush, your socks, your vision, cupboards with dishes, food in the refrigerator, and little gadgets. What things would you miss if you didn't have them?

If you can breathe, swallow, and move your toes, you're indeed fortunate. If you can think, make decisions, and read a book, you're totally blessed. If someone loves you and you have someone to love, that's amazing. Being grateful every day for all things, large and small, will make you a happier person.

Be thankful your pencil can write, you have a lid for the jar of pickles, you have a toilet that can flush and a broom to sweep the floor. Be grateful you have clean clothes, a chair to sit upon, a mind that can think, water when you turn on the faucet, and songs that make you happy. We usually don't think of these things as unusual, but if we didn't have them, we surely would want them. What other things can you be grateful for?

Being grateful for the little things will help you forget your worries, understand how good your life is, and bring more happiness to the world. You will never run out of things to be grateful for. Never.

CHAPTER 17:
BROWSING IN THE HOBBY SHOP

Just a few days after going to the Simmons house for dinner and finding out that they are the owners of the hobby shop downtown, Grandma told John, Grace, and me that she will drive us there to browse.

Browse around? What on earth does that mean? No buying anything? She wasn't clear.

But I didn't want to have her explain and find out. Anyhow, I didn't have any money to spend. I gave it away to Dad for Mom's piano.

John had money that he had saved from taking care of a neighbor's puppy while they were out of town. I don't even know how John meets these people; I obviously haven't met as many people as he has here in Maple River.

Grandma tells me that John sows and reaps, and that's why he has more friends than me. When I asked Grandma what sowing and reaping means, she told me about farmers who plant corn in the spring. A cup of corn seeds produces many ears of corn on the cob. She says that I can plant seeds as John does.

Then Grace said, "It's time, Molly Jo! Grandma is taking us to the hobby store." She was wearing her pink dress and grabbed her purse, crammed with pennies and nickels. She was dancing in the kitchen, waiting to go.

Grandma got her keys and her big blue handbag. Mom told us to listen to Grandma while we were out. I sat up front with Grandma in the car; John and Grace sat in the back. Grandma had written the instructions for getting to the hobby store and wanted me to read them to her.

"Turn left from Pine Grove Drive onto Main Street," I told Grandma.

Grandma said, "Uh-huh."

"Now go straight for three miles."

Grandma said, "Uh-huh." And I saw her glance at her speedometer, but I wasn't sure why.

Grandma said, "When the odometer says 923.6, then we will have gone three miles."

"Oh!"

Then I said, "Turn right onto Chapman Street."

Grandma says, "Molly Jo, I cannot turn right until the odometer says 923.6. Otherwise, we are not following our directions."

"I know that, Grandma! I was just giving you instructions in advance."

Grandma said, "Uh-huh."

When the odometer read 923.6, Grandma saw the sign for Chapman Street. She turned right, and there in all its glory was Simmons Hobby Shop on the right. They had a blue sign in the window that was flashing and said, "Come in."

Grandma parked down the street from it. She could have parked much closer, but she believes that walking is good for us. She tries to log at least one mile every day.

Grace and John jumped out of the car right away and started hurrying toward the store. Grandma called them back and said, "I know you want to skedaddle, but let's stick together. In other words, please slow down."

Drawing by Ashlyn Lindow

I like it when John acts his age sometimes.

I couldn't believe our very own neighbors owned this store. I wondered if they would know us when we walked in. And what if they don't?

When we entered the door, a bell rang. A nice lady with long brown hair in a fancy braid, wearing an apron and a dust cloth in her hand said, "Hello and welcome to Simmons Hobby Shop." She asked if we had been here before and if we needed help with anything. John and Grace told her what they were interested in, and then Grandma spoke up and said, "Thank you, but we are just browsing today."

I couldn't believe it. Grandma repeated that phrase: browsing, we're just browsing. So now it's positive that we aren't buying anything. Not only me but all of us kids. We are just browsing.

John and Grace weren't listening hard enough to pick up on what Grandma was saying.

The nice lady told us she had a coupon for 25% off one item and that each of us could use the coupon - a lot of good for us when we are just browsing.

I began checking around for the calligraphy pens, and Grandma took Grace to admire the stickers. I was sure that John was gazing at the rock collection area when I heard a deep voice from the back of the store say, "Maybe you could guide them around the store." He was speaking to the nice lady.

Oh, oh, oh! It was Mr. Simmons, and I am sure he knows who we are. He told the nice lady up front that we are the Daisys.

And she said, "The Daisys?"

And he said, "Yes, they moved here all the way from Nashville, Tennessee, and they are our super kind new neighbors."

Wow, I didn't know he liked us that much, but he was sincere. He stretched his hand out to Grandma and said, "Oh, you must be Grandma Daisy. Such a pleasure to meet you."

And Grandma said, "Likewise. It's our pleasure to be your neighbors. We came to browse because we've heard such good things about your hobby shop."

"Please browse to your heart's content. Kelly will show you around the store, so you know the lay of the land. I'll be sure to have her show John where the rock hounds meet and show Grace where all our stickers are. And, of course, I know that Molly Jo wants to see the calligraphy area. That's Darla's favorite part of our store!"

Grandma said, "Thank you. You are so gracious to provide us such attention."

Mr. Simmons said, "Only the best for our top-notch customers and friends."

Kelly asked Mr. Simmons, "Should I also show them the new selection of kendamas we have now?"

"Why, that's a great idea, Kelly. Yes, please!"

Ken what? What did she say? None of us had a clue what she was babbling about.

So, Kelly showed us through the store. Rows and rows of cars and trucks, airplanes, helicopters, boats, models, puzzles, rockets, games, and then we came upon the calligraphy section.

I hoped I could just stay right here with the fancy pens and papers. But Kelly said, "How about I show you the rest of the store, and then you can browse as much as you'd like?"

"Okay, sure," Grandma said.

And then she showed us the stickers and educational books and markers. Grace tugged on Grandma's dress, begging her to let her look at the stickers and markers. Grandma agreed. And Kelly told John she had one more thing to show him. She invited me to come along too.

"Okay, sure!" I said.

That's when she said the word "kendamas" again.

"Let's take a gander at the new kendamas that just arrived today."

John said, "Molly Jo, those are the toys that the kids play with at school. Haven't you seen them?"

"No, John, I am not sure what you mean."

"Well, wait till you see. Kendamas are fun to play with."

Then Kelly showed us where they are. All kinds of kendamas in sealed plastic boxes. Grandma overheard John's excitement and came over to explore.

"Oh! Those are like the cup and ball games I played as a young girl. They must be back in style."

John said, "Do you know what a kendama is, Grandma?"

"Well, I do now!" Grandma said. "And they are so fun."

Kelly let John practice with one. He really didn't do so well on his first try. The ball never landed in the cup. Kelly gave him a quick lesson. "Hold it like this and bend at your knees."

Then she showed us a few tricks she could do with the kendama. And I mean she is fantastic!

She smiled and said, "I work in a hobby shop so I can practice a lot. Repetition is the secret. You'll get good at it too if you just practice over and over like me. It will improve your balance and your hand and eye coordination."

John kept trying to get the ball into the cup. Kelly told him to keep his wrists straight and not to scoop for the ball.

She said, "Let the kendama do the work for you."

John just kept trying.

Grandma said we could all have a few more minutes to browse in the hobby shop. Grace found stickers with teddy bears on them, while John continued playing with the kendama. I couldn't believe he didn't even check out the rock or bug collection stuff. I liked the fancy pens and paper I found but wasn't sure how to use them.

Soon it was time to go, and Grace had this longing puppy-dog look on her face, which Dad sometimes has. She showed Grandma the stickers she found, and Grandma said, "Those are very special, Grace."

"May I get them, Grandma?"

"We are just browsing today, Grace."

"But please, Grandma?"

Kelly added, "She could use her 25% coupon on them."

"That's true," Grandma said. "Maybe all three children can get one item each today."

Grace started to jump up and down like she does when she gets excited.

John said, "The kendama? May I get it, Grandma?"

"Only if you promise to practice with it, John."

"I promise, Grandma. I will practice every day. I will learn from kids at school, too."

"What about you, Molly Jo?" Grandma asked me.

"I'm not sure what I want, Grandma. I like pens and paper, but not sure."

"Okay, we can come back another day, and maybe you will find something special," Grandma said.

Kelly said, "We have some new calligraphy books with pretty alphabets in them. Would you like to see those?"

"Yes, please."

I found a book that shows how to draw super curly letters. "This is the best, Grandma. May I get this book?"

"If you promise to practice your calligraphy, Molly Jo."

"I promise, Grandma. I will practice every day. I will write letters to Melissa using the curly letters."

"Then, we are ready to be checked out, Kelly. Each of them has found something special!"

I thanked Grandma for letting each of us get something we enjoyed. She didn't have to do that. We are fortunate kids.

Kelly placed each of our items in separate red bags with "Simmons Hobby Shop" stamped on them and a picture of their store. Mr. Simmons came up from the back and wondered if we all found something we genuinely wanted. We all said a resounding yes!

"And how about Grandma?" he asked.

Oh, dear, Grandma has nothing yet. We can't leave without Grandma getting something too.

"She loves reading books," I told him.

Mr. Simmons said, "I absolutely know what she will love. Just two doors down from us, in the cutest little shop you will ever see, is Eliza's Corner Café and Second-Hand Book Store. Arrange a day when you can spend an hour or two, and you'll see why I am so excited for you to go there."

Drawing by
Ashlyn Lindow

"Okay, Mr. Simmons. That sounds dandy to me. When a family is new in town, like ours, it's helpful to get ideas from people who've lived here a long time," Grandma said.

"You can call me Chuck. My real name is Charles, but I go by Chuck. And yes, there are so many delightful places to enjoy in Maple River."

Has the Daisy family been to the Maple River Sweet Shop? If you have a sweet tooth, it will become your favorite place. I promise. I visit there too often myself, but Darla doesn't mind when I bring home a bag of handmade saltwater taffy.

And don't forget Maine Maple Sunday, the fourth Sunday in March. Your whole family can sample pure fresh maple syrup from right here in Maine."

Drawing by Millie Virginia Morris

"You bestow some excellent suggestions, Mr. Simmons, I mean Chuck. Thank you, Chuck, for your extra kind service to us. We'll be back. Your hobby shop is a treasure in the heart of downtown Maple River," said Grandma.

Just then, out of the corner of my eye, I saw something I can't explain. I suddenly felt my heart pounding.

Right next to the checkout stand was a display of many books – that look identical to my secret book. I got closer and – oh my goodness – the cover is exactly like the book I found in my closet. *Advice for a Remarkable Life*

How can there be more than one of these secret books? I thought I had the only one in the world. I tried not to let anyone see me glance at them, but Mr. Simmons noticed.

He said, "I see you noticed my display of books, Molly Jo. Would you like to get one today? It will become your new favorite book. I am sure because I wrote it myself."

"Uh, uh, uh. You wrote this book yourself? Wow!"

"Well, yes. I hope that's not a big surprise, Molly Jo. All my life, I've been a thinker and a writer.

Darla tells me I'm something else. Personally, I think I'm an exceptional thought leader."

"Uh, huh! Let's plan next time, Mr. Simmons."

I cannot tell him I already have one of those secret books. Not even Grandma knows that.

Grace said, "Molly Jo, that looks like the book we ..."

And I quickly interrupted her and told Grandma it's time to check out. We kids are starving. That was a close call!

Keep a Daily Journal
Advice for a Remarkable Life

When you look back at your life someday, there will be things you wished you had done. Writing in a journal may be one of them. A daily journal will eventually become a treasure if you keep it going.

Writing in a journal doesn't mean you need to spend a lot of time on it. If you would just write a sentence or two a day, you'll be surprised how fun it will be later to go back and read it. You don't need a fancy journal; you can even find them at the dollar store.

What are some things you could include in your journal? You might write what you did that day – perhaps something unusual happened. You could draw something cool or tell a joke. A long time from now, whatever you write in your journal will be fascinating to read, mainly if you include a few details. For example, if you write down that you rode your bike, maybe tell where you traveled or what your bicycle looks like.

You might describe your favorite song or mention the book you're reading. How about including something surprising you learned in school or divulging what you are secretly wishing for? You could explain how you celebrated a holiday or vacation. Somedays, instead of writing in your journal, you could attach a ticket to an event you attended, a sales receipt for something you bought, a flower you picked, or a photo of something that you appreciate. A journal is your story because you are significant. Capture your daily memories and thoughts in a journal and include today's date for each entry you write.

CHAPTER 18:
LETTER #2 FROM MELISSA

The next day after school, John and I raced in from the bus. The aroma of Mom's sugar cookies traveled through the whole house. I couldn't believe she made them for us, the best day ever. Flour, sugar, and cookie dough covered the kitchen table.

What I love most about these cookies is the grape jelly in the center of the cookie. Right before Mom bakes them, she uses her thumb to make a little indentation in the cookie's center. Then she spoons a bit of jelly into the thumbprint and sprinkles sugar all over the cookie's top. When they bake, the jam becomes a part of the cookie.

John wondered if he could invite his friend William to try the cookies and play. Mom said, "Sure, as long as you get your homework completed by seven tonight."

John said, "I will, I will!" And off he went charging to see if William was home.

Mom told me I had another letter from Melissa in the mail. There it was, on the kitchen table, looking at me. I was sort of giggly inside to see it, but my face felt red because I hadn't yet answered her first letter. Why don't I finish things? I started to write to her, but Grandma says it's not the start, but the finish that really matters.

Melissa had addressed the envelope in her fancy lettering, and I began reading.

Dear Molly Jo,

I hope you liked the little gift I sent in the last letter. I can't wait to hear from you. Things aren't the same here without you. I miss you so much! I have some great news to tell you. I was thinking this would be a surprise, but my parents said I could tell you.

When it's our autumn break in October, Mom and Dad are driving us to Maine for a vacation, and we will visit you. Can you believe it, Molly Jo?

We will leave on a Saturday morning and get to your place on Tuesday night. We are stopping in Boston before we get to your home. Mom says you have school the next day, but we'll do some sightseeing while you're at school.

I wish you had an autumn break then too, Molly Jo, but we can see each other lots in the evenings! Isn't it simply great? I've never been to Maple River.

Your Mom and Dad know about our trip - they were keeping it a secret from you. I can't wait for October to get here, Molly Jo.

Love...Melissa xoxoxo

I can hardly believe that Melissa is coming to Maine.

"Mom, Melissa's family is coming to our house in October!"

"I know, Molly Jo. It's been hard not to tell you, but isn't it just the best? It will be a good time. I am so glad Melissa's letter arrived because I was busting at the seams to tell you."

"I need to study my calligraphy book and write Melissa back today, Mom."

"Well, good, Molly Jo. It's about time! Melissa will love that, and so will Grandma."

Then John and William came barreling in the screen door wanting cookies.

Please don't let the boys eat all of them.

CHAPTER 19:
MELISSA'S FAMILY VISITS MAPLE RIVER

I don't think about being new every single minute, like when we first arrived. A few weeks have passed, and I am getting in the groove here, which is a total shock.

My head is funny, so let me explain. I think in two directions now – both forward and backward. When we first got here, I only thought about things backward. I missed everything behind me – my house, my school, and my friends in Tennessee.

Now, my brain likes looking ahead as well. Like when will we get to go back to Aunt Jane's House? And when will we visit Boston or try the blueberry ice cream at the Maple River Ice Cream Shop?

I cannot wait until Melissa's family comes to see us. Just a few days left. I have been crossing off each day on the calendar on my bedroom wall.

Mom told me she borrowed a cot from the Simmons family so that Melissa could sleep with Grace and me. Grace likes the cot so much that she told Mom that she would sleep in that, and Melissa could use her bed.

"Why, of course, Grace. That will work out perfectly!"

Grace held tightly onto Smokey and said, "I just can't wait for Melissa's family to get here."

Mom and Dad will let Melissa's parents sleep in their room. And they will sleep downstairs. Melissa's family will get to stay until Saturday morning!

I asked Ms. Jewel if I could bring Melissa to school with me one day, and she said, "That would be fantastic!

Seldom do we get a guest from Tennessee in our classroom."

I hope Melissa doesn't mind going to school one day of her fall break. I don't think she will mind because she will get to be with me, and I will get to be with her. And she will get to learn what my school is all about. My head is just swirling with fantastic ideas.

Monday came, and I went to school like any other day, but it wasn't just any old Monday. It was the day before Melissa's family arrived. When I got home from school, there was plenty to do to get the house ready for their visit.

Grandma not only dusted everything in sight but also washed windows and painted the front porch. Dad built a new porch swing for our porch, and Grandma sewed new covers for the cushions. And Mom decorated the porch with planters, even though it will be freezing in a few weeks. She said that they were on clearance.

John cleaned his room, which only happens once a year, and he even sprayed his room with a minty spray that Grandma let him borrow. He is almost as excited as me. Grace made a big sign on the front door for Melissa's family that says, "Welcome!" I wrote it in pencil, and she used her crayons to make it colorful. Even the Simmons family was excited for us. They have heard so much about Melissa's family that they practically know them.

Mom wrote out a menu for the meals we'd have while they are here. The first night she is making a pot roast and pumpkin bars. It will be just like old times with all of us jabbering in the kitchen. I cannot wait to show Melissa around our new house. My heart is about to burst right out of my body.

Tuesday morning arrived, and I begged Mom to let me stay home from school.

"Please, please, please let me stay home!"

"Molly Jo, Melissa's family won't be here until dinner time. You'll have time after school to do any other preparations you want. For example, get your homework done. Hint, hint."

So off to school John and I went. Ms. Jewel knew I could hardly contain my excitement. She announced to the class that I would bring my friend Melissa to school the next day. This day lasted forever. I kept checking the clock. 10 am, 10:15 am, 11:00 am, noon, and then afternoon arrived. Holy potato chips!

When I got home from school, Grace taped up more welcome signs. Mom had the pot roast cooking in the slow cooker, and Dad was already back from Daisy Designs. John practiced his kendama, and Mrs. Simmons dropped off a giant red tin with butterscotch cookies for us to have this week. I hope with all my heart, they are better than her pizza sauce. And she also brought over a bouquet of orange and yellow mums from her garden.

The phone rang. Mom said, "Hello!"

I could tell it was Melissa's Mom.

Mom said, "You're arriving a little sooner than expected? Oh! It can't be too soon for us. We are all ready for you."

When Mom hung up, she said they will be here in fifteen minutes.

I ran through the house, seeing if there's anything else I needed to do. John took out the trash. I sprayed

Grandma's minty air freshener in every single room. Mom put on a pot of coffee, and Dad was pacing the floors.

I kept checking the front door, spying to see if their green van was here yet.

Mom said, "It's like waiting for water to boil."

Soon I heard a horn honking and their van pulling into our driveway. I was trembling, but for a good reason! I stared out the screen door, and they were pulling a moving trailer behind their van. What? Are they moving here? Oh my gosh, can this wild dream be real?

We all ran out, and the hugging was non-stop. Our family has missed Melissa's family even more than I can say! I am so grateful they took this long journey to see us.

I couldn't help but blurt out, "Are you moving here, Melissa?"

"Oh no, Molly Jo. We aren't moving here."

"But why do you have the trailer behind your van?"

"Your Dad knows why we brought that with us. I promised to keep it a secret."

"A secret? Dad, why do they have a moving trailer with them?" I asked.

"There's something extraordinary in that trailer, Molly Jo. It's a present for your Mom."

I couldn't wait to see what it was!

Melissa's Dad said, "Shall we?"

And Dad nodded his head. He told Mom to turn around and shut her eyes. So, she did.

They unlocked the back of the trailer and rolled up the back door. And inside, there was something huge that was wrapped up with heavy blankets and tied with straps. Melissa's Dad unbuckled the straps, took off the blankets, and there, right there, was Mom's piano!

How in the world is that possible? How did that happen? Oh, the lightbulb came on in my brain.

Melissa's family has been keeping Mom's piano all this time. I cannot believe I never guessed this. Why did I think we'd never see her piano again?

I thought my head would pop – seeing her piano here in our driveway was so breathtaking. Melissa is the best secret keeper. She never gave me even the tiniest hint.

But, now that I think about it, my secret book is right! We already had what we need. We had Mom's piano all along but didn't realize it.

Dad said to Mom, "You can peek now."

She turned around, saw her long-lost piano, and just burst out crying.

Dad said, "It's been tough for me to keep this secret all this time."

Melissa said, "Me too. It's been so hard not to tell Molly Jo."

Mom gave a huge bear hug to Melissa's family and said, "What can I say except thank you! I never imagined seeing my piano again."

Melissa's Dad says, "Well, why don't we get your piano inside so it will be back home again?"

Dad said, "Sure! Let's do it! John, you can help us."

Suddenly, I realized that we could have a caroling party for Christmas! We can invite the Simmons family! And maybe Anna Lin's family! And William's family!

The guys hauled our heavy piano from the trailer, onto the driveway, up the front porch steps, and into our living room. Watching them was a nail-biter. They parked the piano on our big long wall where we didn't have any furniture yet. Perfect!

"Ah, my piano is home now!" Mom said while taking in a big sigh of relief.

Having the piano back makes it really feel like home again.

Our family gave Melissa's family the grand tour of our house as the sun was setting on Pine Grove Drive.

That night I found an envelope on my bed with $40.00 in it from Dad. He wrote this letter to me that I will forever keep.

Dear Molly Jo,

You have a heart of gold to contribute your money to Mom's piano fund. I didn't want to tell you about the piano being kept at Melissa's house. I wanted to be sure that Mom was thoroughly surprised when her piano arrived. But your generous heart is the best of all.

Thank you, daughter. You make Mom and me enormously proud. You are one exceptional girl, just like Grandma always tells you.

I love you. For your kind heart, I added a little extra money to round it up to $40.

Love,
Dad xo

Somehow, someway, at this very minute, living here in Maple River is feeling ok. It's not the same as Nashville, and I still miss so much there, but my family is here, and I am at home. I love my sweet Nashville, but I am *never looking back* with a sad heart anymore. I'm clearly a girl with two hometowns that I love.

I will use part of my money to treat Melissa to ice cream this week. I will share some with Grandma to get tea at Eliza's Corner Café. And I will share the rest with John for his drone fund.

I hope this week lasts forever with Melissa's family because I don't ever want to say goodbye again.

CHAPTER 20:
SAYING GOODBYE ONE MORE TIME

To my sad but knowing heart, after a week of fun beyond belief, Saturday morning arrived. We got to do so many things: take Melissa to my school, visit downtown Maple River for ice cream, introduce Rudy to Melissa's family, and build some birdhouses for Cherry Forest.

My only regret is that Melissa and Anna Lin didn't get to meet each other. Melissa never needs to worry that she will be replaced by another best friend, but I do love them both.

Melissa and her parents were darting all over the house, gathering their things. This morning they are leaving to drive back to Nashville.

Mom said, "Don't forget to check the bathroom shower and the nightstands in the bedroom."

Dad said, "Don't forget the extra shoes and jackets you brought by the front door."

And Grace shouted, "Don't forget to take the signs I made for you!"

Melissa's Mom said, "We'd never forget those, Grace. They're the best, and they mean so much to us!"

Grandma said, "Please don't forget to pack the little goody bags I made for your trip back."

Grandma gathered snacks for their family and a little goody bag for each of them from Maple River. I like what she got Melissa: some colorful fabric with bananas from the sewing store and a book cover pattern. Melissa loves my Grandma! And the material has bananas on it because Melissa loves to call her "Grandma Banana," which makes Grandma chuckle.

Dad was outside jabbering to Melissa's Dad. They were figuring out when our families would see each other again. Mom said I could invite Melissa to come up next summer to go to the beach with us, and I have a sneaky hunch that her parents will let her. Now that would be the best thing ever! And we might even have a treehouse by then.

When it was time for Melissa's family to leave, Mom gave an envelope to her parents, and Melissa's Mom tucked it into her purse. I bet it was a thank you for bringing our piano to Maine.

Their family visit was a miracle to me because I never realized how much her family misses us. It's almost as much as we miss them, and I didn't even know that was possible!

Melissa rushed up to me as she was packing her last few things. She said, "I wish I could live in Maple River, too, Molly Jo!"

Really? I never ever, ever thought she would say that. Would she want to leave Nashville on purpose? How in the world would any kid want to move away from Chesterfield Lane? I thought my head would pop off when she said that.

Grandma said, "See Molly Jo? You've inspired Melissa to be adventuresome. She wants to be like you! Of course, she loves Chesterfield Lane. We all do and always will, but she sees there are other wonderful places too."

Our two families didn't say goodbye for long because that would have made it harder. I know I'll be seeing Melissa again, maybe even next summer for our trip to the beach.

I am so glad she got to see my new house and my new hometown.

Now, if only we could get their family to come here and stay. That would be the cat's pajamas.

I now know that happiness is a decision that I can make for myself every day. Even without Melissa living across the street from me, I can decide to be happy.

Never Give Up
Advice for a Remarkable Life

When you're trying hard to do something good, but it isn't working out, what do you do? You keep trying. You hang in there. You be persistent and never give up. That's what you do.

Anyone who has achieved something significant had to go through days when it was hard or seemed impossible. But they kept working at it, kept trying different things, continued learning, and didn't allow anything to get in their way. They never give up.

It's good to have a stubborn attitude sometimes, dig in your heels, and not give up on something worthwhile. The road to achievement usually isn't easy. You must go around roadblocks and pick yourself up when you're dirty.

It's so easy to say that something is "too hard." For sure, some things are hard, and some days might feel overwhelming. But if what you're trying to do is meaningful to you, then keep trying. Rise above the obstacles!

A healthy baby learning to walk doesn't give up, even though it isn't easy at first. Their legs are wobbly, and balancing is hard. Babies don't mind when they fall over and over again. Wouldn't it be sad if a baby said, "Walking is too hard," and they decided they would simply crawl for the rest of their life?

You have the power to never give up. Will you put it to good use?

CHAPTER 21:
THE MAPLE RIVER PROJECT

Mom invited the Simmons family to come to our house for dinner because she says it's nice to return the favor. It's our turn to treat them.

I didn't expect it would unfold like I am about to tell you.

Mom made herb-roasted chicken and homemade potato salad, which are two of my absolute favorite foods in the world. She sliced cucumbers and carrots with her fancy crinkle cutter. She asked me to arrange them on Grandma's beautiful crystal platter.

Mom also asked me to set the table with our blue cloth napkins and our Sunday dinnerware. Wow, this will be a deluxe dinner, not an ordinary-middle-of-the-week meal like we usually have.

Mom said, "The Simmons family treated us like royalty at their house for pizza, so let's show them a good time at our house."

Dad even came home early from the woodshop and changed into his better clothes. He never does that! Well, he changes his clothes, but hardly ever comes home from work early on a weeknight.

The Simmons family arrived right on time at 6 pm. I could hear them coming from across the street – that deep voice and jovial laugh of Mr. Simmons is hard to mistake for anyone else.

Mr. Simmons never disappoints; he wore his yellow plaid pants with his red socks and a light blue shirt. I wondered if he only wears this outfit for us. Or is it his favorite outfit?

I hope Dad doesn't start dressing that way. He wouldn't, would he?

When they arrived at our front door, Mom and Dad answered it, and there were plenty of hellos and hugs. Mrs. Simmons held a heavy black skillet with potholders on each hand.

She gave Dad the skillet and said, "Be mighty careful."

"Oh, Darla, it smells heavenly," and Dad set it on the kitchen counter.

Mrs. Simmons said, "It's my homemade apple crisp that I make every fall for Chuck."

Dad said, "I bet it would go well with that vanilla ice cream we have in the freezer."

Mr. Simmons chuckled. "Perfecto Mundo."

And he had a brown bag with something inside that he gave to Mom. He said, "Fix the kids some sandwiches with this. They will love it. Such a long-time tradition here in Maine."

She opened the bag and found a jar of marshmallow fluff.

"Uh, thank you, Chuck. You want me to make marshmallow sandwiches for the kids?"

He chuckled his big belly laugh and said, "Once in a while, make fluffernutter sandwiches. It's a New England specialty; I grew up with fluffernutter."

"Fluffernutter sandwiches, Chuck?"

"Yes, that's it. Spread peanut butter on one slice of bread and marshmallow fluff on the other slice, and then slap the two slices together. You will have the best gooey fluffernutter sandwich in the world – much like a PB & J but with marshmallow fluff. And if you want to take it one step further, go for a grilled fluffernutter sandwich. It will knock your socks off."

Mom said, "Uh, huh. Thank you, Chuck. We'll do that soon."

Grandma's eyebrows went straight up, and she shook her head in disbelief. "A banana & butter sandwich is just as tasty and more nutritious for children, Mr. Simmons. I mean, Chuck."

"Yes, Grandma, but nothing like fluffernutter. Kids love it!" he said, laughing in his big loud way. "And if you spread a gob of marshmallow fluff between two flat pieces of chocolate cake, you've made yourself a Whoopie Pie!"

Oh, so finally, I know what a Whoopie Pie is. I am loving this funny guy, Mr. Simmons.

Mr. Simmons also brought a red folder and set it on the foyer table. The letters "MRP" were written on it, and I wondered what that could mean. He saw me glancing at it and told me he would explain it all tonight.

Grandma was prepping in the kitchen, wearing her green apron, and slicing a crusty loaf of sourdough bread from the bakery. Mr. Simmons told Mrs. Simmons, "I had the good fortune to meet Grandma at the hobby shop last week."

And Mrs. Simmons said, "Oh, Chuck, you beat me to it! So nice to meet you, Grandma".

I thought it so funny that they both called her Grandma. She's not their grandma.

Dinner was ready, and we all gathered around our table, with Stephen wanting to be next to John. Mom arranged flowers and candles on the table. Dad said a short prayer, and it was time for Simple Joys around the table. The Simmons family doesn't know about Simple Joys, but they joined in anyhow.

Mr. Simmons said, "My Simple Joy is catching the squirrels congregating under our bird feeder every day. I release them into the woods down by the lake."

Mrs. Simmons said, "Oh Chuck, you shouldn't be sharing those things. The Daisys will think we're bad people catching squirrels. Besides that, it's not legal in Maple River city limits."

Mr. Simmons rolled his eyes and said, "Oh Darla, we don't mistreat the squirrels one tiny bit. In fact, we give them a lakefront home. If that's the worst thing we do, then I dare say we're angels!"

Mrs. Simmons shook her head. She rested her finger on the side of her head and thought for a moment. Then she took in a big breath and said, "My Simple Joy was cleaning closets today and donating plaid pants to the thrift store."

She said, "I held the plaid pants in my lap and wondered if they brought joy to my heart. Nope, they don't, so I dropped them into the donation bag."

Uh-oh. The room fell dead silent.

Dad stared at Mom, and Mom stared at Dad. Mr. Simmons dropped his jaw and took in a big deep breath.

We all knew what we were thinking. Bye-bye, plaid pants. Too bad, Mr. Simmons.

Mom broke the silence and said, "Grandma, it's your turn for your Simple Joy."

"Oh, yes!" she said. "Having the Simmons family over for dinner is my Simple Joy. And I hope I can see the wooden giraffe in their living room someday."

Thank heavens for Grandma. She knows just the right thing to say and when to say it.

Then we started passing the herb-roasted chicken, Mom's excellent potato salad, and roasted veggies. Grandma got the breadbasket rolling too. This food gives me happy feet; it's better than pizza with fennel sauce a hundred million times.

Mr. Simmons ate two extra servings of roasted chicken, which made Mom's eyes twinkle. And Mrs. Simmons wondered if Mom would share her potato salad recipe. I must have been staring off into space because Mom kicked my foot under the table. She said, "Molly Jo, Mrs. Simmons just asked you how school is going."

"Oh, oh, yes, Mrs. Simmons. I am getting used to it."

Mrs. Simmons asked, "Is school here anything like Nashville?"

John blurted out, "It's fun because we get to ride the bus." And Grace said, "I want to ride the bus too."

Dad explained to Mr. Simmons all about Daisy Designs and how he and Uncle Jim work together in the woodshop at Uncle Jim's house. I could tell that Mr. Simmons didn't know much about building things, but he listened carefully to every word Dad spoke as if his ears were glued on Dad.

Mom said, "Kids, let's clear the table so we can have dessert soon."

Grandma got up from her chair to help, and Mom said, "No, no, no, Grandma. You relax and let the kids do it." Grandma sat right back down with a huff; she prefers helping.

Mr. Simmons got up to grab that red folder and rushed back to the table with it. He cupped his hands to the side of his mouth and privately asked Mom and Dad if he could have a few minutes to talk about it.

Mom said, "Well, sure you can!"

Dad said, "Take it away, Chuck."

Mr. Simmons said, "Molly Jo, how about you join us too?"

Me? Why did he want me to hear this and not the other kids? Mr. Simmons said the other kids could hear about it another time but let them go play. I wasn't sure if I should feel proud or disappointed.

He opened the folder and pulled out a stack of orange flyers that said, "Maple River Project." Mr. Simmons said that he oversees the committee that welcomes new families to Maple River.

Grandma said, "Oh, that's a great idea to welcome new families here."

Mr. Simmons said, "Yes, our town is friendly, and we love having new people make Maple River their hometown."

I wondered what this has to do with me. I mean, I'm just a kid.

"Molly Jo," said Mr. Simmons in his deep, loud voice. "I spoke with your parents and Grandma earlier and asked them if I could invite you to join our project, and they said you might like to be a part of it."

"Uh, huh, I am not sure, Mr. Simmons."

"Well, your parents told me about the project you completed in Tennessee – baking cookies and taking them to the hospital for sick children. And I thought to myself, how many ten-year-old girls are as ambitious as you? You are a natural leader, Molly Jo."

"Well, maybe," I said with a little tremble in my voice and just going along with what he said.

"We are hoping for a young person to come up with a great idea of a way to welcome new families to our town. Something we can deliver to them or something we can do for them. Would you reflect on this, Molly Jo?"

Dad said, "Molly Jo, this is such a great opportunity. You are a creative girl. You're a cookie baker, you enjoy writing little books, you love calligraphy, you're fond of artsy and how-to stuff, you have a big heart, and well, I could go on and on."

And Mom followed by saying, "You could enlist help from your new friends here, like your friend Anna Lin, who is also new to Maple River."

I guess I could, but I didn't want to say it out loud because that means I will. And I am not ready to answer!

Mrs. Simmons said, "As soon as I discovered you enjoy calligraphy, Molly Jo, I knew that you'd be a wonderful girl to come up with ideas for this project. We calligraphers are creative, aren't we?"

"Uh, yes, I think we are, Mrs. Simmons," I said as I shrugged my shoulders.

Grandma boldly said in her I'm-so-certain voice, "You don't even know all the things that Molly Jo is capable of. She's a modest girl. But being new to Maple River, she knows what it feels like to move here. And my Molly Jo Daisy is one great worker. You'd be hard-pressed to find a better girl for the job."

"Well, let's get that apple crisp out, and I'll dish up some ice cream with it," Dad said.

I was glad Dad switched the subject so I could breathe. My heart was pounding hard.

Tasting Mrs. Simmons' apple crisp topped with a scoop of vanilla ice cream was the best dessert I can ever remember in my whole life.

Mrs. Simmons said, "Those apples came right from our backyard, Molly Jo. But the real secret about my recipe is the Maple River Spice Mix I sprinkle on top."

Mom's ears perked up.

"Spice mix? Maple River Spice Mix? Where might I get some of that, Darla?" Mom requested as she raised up in her chair.

Mrs. Simmons said, "I can fix you right up."

Dad said, "Good, we need some of that around here."

I didn't understand how I became the center of this Maple River Project, but I will consider it. Could I be good enough for it? It's an honor to be chosen, but who am I to welcome new people when I am a new person myself?

When it was time for the Simmons to go home, I saw Mr. Simmons whisper to Mrs. Simmons. I think he wondered if she had given a pair of his plaid pants to the thrift store today.

"Of course not, Chuck!" she said in a very-sure-almost-surprised-and-a-little mad voice. "I gave away my plaid pants. You know I wouldn't donate your plaid pants without your permission first."

Hmm. Was I the only one who thought it was a Mr. Simmons' pants she gave away? Now that was a close call for him.

On the way out the door, Mrs. Simmons said, "Grandma, would you like to come over and meet Rudy?"

"Rudy? Why I'd love to meet Rudy. But who's Rudy?" Grandma asked.

"Oh, he's our giraffe that Molly Jo told you about. Didn't I tell you his name before? His name is Rudy."

Grandma clapped her hands and took no time putting on her sweater and bunny slippers. Mrs. Simmons invited everyone who wanted to see Rudy the giraffe again.

No way was I going to stay behind, and how in the world did I not know Rudy's name before?

I wanted to see Grandma's face when she sees Rudy for the first time. And I want her to see the Simmons perfect house with everything perfectly lined up and sparkling with amazing colors and all its fanciness.

CHAPTER 22:
GRANDMA MEETS RUDY

When we got there, Mr. Simmons tapped on some lamps because it had gotten dark. Did you hear what I said? He tapped on the lamps. He simply touched them, and they magically turned on. If I could ask for anything for my next birthday, it would be a lamp just like that.

Once again, I saw their nicer-than-furniture-store living room I so vividly remembered. The shoes at the front door were lined up in a row, from Mr. Simmons boat-size shoes down to Stephen's small cowboy boots, and that blue velvet couch and silver coffee table – so beautiful! And no magazines or toys lying anywhere. Absolutely spotless!

The room was overflowing with the fragrance of flowers from a little machine that puffs steam into the air. Oh, please, will my parents notice all this extreme loveliness that I wished we had?

Mrs. Simmons stretched her arm to point to their adorable, crazy-tall Rudy, standing next to the pillar. She said, "Grandma, please go over and behold our simply marvelous friend. Just pour over his cuteness."

As Grandma inched over, she crisscrossed her heart with both hands and did a little curtsy. Then she exclaimed, "My heavens, he's more astonishing than I could have imagined. Oh, the details in his face, in fact, everywhere. I just love him, Darla!"

Grandma's eyes were more sparkly than my jars of glitter. I know she is just as pleased as punch.

Mrs. Simmons proudly said, "We've only had him for a few months, Grandma, and we simply adore him!"

Grandma said, "But, may I ask a big question? Where did you ever get such an exciting creation for your home? I've never seen the likes of this beautiful giraffe named Rudy."

Mr. Simmons interrupted before Mrs. Simmons could even spit out a word, as he often does.

"Well, that's an easy question to answer, Grandma. The young boy Christopher, who used to live in your house before your family arrived, created Rudy with the help of his Dad, who is a woodcarver. Before they left our neighborhood, they gave him to our family as a gift. They built Rudy from cedar fence posts that we took down when we got our new aluminum fence. Our cedar fence was beyond repair.

"Christopher's Dad carved the overall shape, and Christopher burnished the features on his face and spots. The thick brown fringe is from carefully wrapped yarn that belonged to Christopher's Mom. Christopher is a highly creative boy. Rudy is a little wabi-sabi, and that's what makes him so real and true to life."

"Well, that's one remarkable story," Grandma said without hesitating.

"In fact, Molly Jo, you and Christopher have a lot in common. You're both go-getters, big-hearted kids," Mr. Simmons said, bellowing in his funny way.

I just nodded, but inside of my head, I wondered who this Christopher boy is. And could he be the Christopher who left his book in my closet?

Mom said, "Molly Jo, Molly, Jo! Earth to Molly Jo," in a rather loud voice.

"Yes?"

"You drifted off somewhere, and we're all leaving now. It's late, and the Simmons want to have the rest of their evening back."

"Oh, yeah, sure, Mom."

So, we all gave quick hugs and said goodnight while Grandma talked non-stop on the way home about Rudy and how special he is. And I asked Mom about their house. About how tidy it is and beautiful. Mom raised one eyebrow and said, "Bless her heart, Molly Jo, but I bet Mrs. Simmons would clean the Grand Canyon if she could."

"She would?"

"Nah, I'm just kidding, Molly Jo. She's a tidy neighbor and an exceedingly kind one, too."

"Mom, my friend Anna Lin says that every time we clean something, we make something else dirty. Is that right?"

"Well, yes and no. It's not a good reason to have a messy room, Molly Jo. But I don't need to tell you that."

And that was the end of our evening.

Be Curious
Advice for a Remarkable Life

Curious people wonder about things and like to explore. Life is more fun when we are inquisitive because we use our imagination and minds to figure things out.

Curious people like to read books, ask questions, watch shows, visit places, and take the time to dig deep to learn more. Being curious makes us more interesting people.

Be curious about your everyday life. Turn a rock over to see what's underneath. Figure out why ice is hard, but water isn't. Wonder how the stars stay in the sky or why babies never give up when they learn to walk.

Another way of being curious is by being interested in other people. If a friend has a garden or a rock collection, ask them about it or take the time to stop by.

Be curious in a friendly way because it makes people feel special. Doesn't it feel good when someone asks you about your hobbies or interests? You feel important and appreciated.

When you are curious, one thing leads to another. For example, if you are curious about why it rains, you might explore different clouds. And when you examine the kinds of clouds, you might study types of storms. And when you read about storms, you might discover places that have hurricanes or tornadoes. Your curious mind will learn so much. It's incredible!

CHAPTER 23:
SATURDAY WITH ANNA LIN

This weekend Anna Lin is coming to our house to play. I am so happy to finally have a friend over!

Grace wonders every day, "Is this the day Anna Lin is coming?" Grace knows about Anna Lin's twirly skirts, and she is hoping Anna Lin wears one to our house. I told Grace that she probably dresses up on school days, not on Saturdays.

Grandma is helping me come up with ideas I can do with Anna Lin. One thought is to bake cookies. Grandma says that's a good start, but she has some other ideas up her sleeves. Why on earth would she have ideas up her sleeves?

"Molly Jo, how about having Anna Lin help you come up with suggestions for the Maple River Project?" Grandma said.

"Oh, Grandma, she will think that's boring!"

"Not if you tell her it's a chance to be creative and become an honored citizen in Maple River. And because you are both new to town, you are quite qualified to come up with suggestions. It's all about the way you tell her," Grandma said.

"Oh, I never thought of it that way, Grandma."

"Maybe, just maybe, there's a way to combine things that you and Anna Lin love to do. For example, you love to do calligraphy and to write stories. Oh, and to bake cookies. What does Anna Lin like to do?"

"Anna Lin draws better than me, and twirling and playing Fish," I said.

"Aha! Anna Lin's drawing plus your calligraphy and writing. Now we're getting somewhere," Grandma said.

"How does that make a good Maple River project?" I asked.

"Well, for sure, we don't know yet, but when Anna Lin comes over, I bet you can come up with some good thoughts while the two of you bake chocolate chip cookies."

Mom overheard Grandma and said, "You can bake extras so that Anna Lin and her family can also enjoy a plate of cookies. That's one way we can welcome her family to Maple River."

John was in the kitchen, and he chimed in by saying that he wants to deliver some cookies to William's family.

"William isn't new to Maple River, John," I said.

"That doesn't matter, Molly Jo. He's my friend, and you don't have to be new to get cookies."

"You're right, John, cookies are good for any reason."

Saturday came, and Grace skipped all over the house. John organized his rock collection and practiced his kendama. The weather was cold and blustery, so windy that your hat would fly away if you are not holding onto it.

Dad asked me to let him know when Anna Lin arrived. He said, "I don't want our screen door to blow off its hinges, Molly Jo, so I will hold it when she gets here."

Anna Lin's Mom doesn't know how to drive, so her Dad drives her to our house. When they arrived, her Dad held Anna Lin's door so she could get out. Anna Lin lugged a tote bag, and it was flapping like crazy in the wind, but she never let go of the handles.

As I watched out the window, I shouted, "Dad, Anna Lin is here."

Dad came right to the door and motioned for them to wait. He held the door handle with both hands so that the wind wouldn't snap the door away. He greeted her by saying, "So you must be Anna Lin. Please come into our warm house."

Anna Lin came in, followed by her Dad, along with a chilling swish of cold air that gave me goosebumps. My Dad and her Dad instantly became friends because they started talking about trucks right away.

Anna Lin and I snuck away to the kitchen without even saying goodbye to her Dad, but we probably should have. Her Dad shouted, "Anna Lin, I will pick you up in three hours."

In the kitchen, Mom and Grandma arranged the ingredients for chocolate chip cookies on the counter. Anna Lin bit her lower lip, and I told her to relax because I've baked cookies before, and it's not that hard. Besides, I said to her that we can munch on the extra chocolate chips, which made her smile and skip around the kitchen.

Anna Lin relaxed more when the grownups allowed us to bake by ourselves. I secretly bet she's never made cookies by herself because of all her questions.

"What's ¼ teaspoon mean, Molly Jo?"

I told her, "You just need a measuring spoon that says ¼ on it, and you fill the ingredient to the top of the spoon. It's a ridiculously small amount, Anna Lin."

"Oh," she said, "That's what those numbers mean on the measuring spoons. Guess I should have known that, Molly Jo."

"Don't worry, Anna Lin. You know things that I don't know so we can learn from each other."

We are not supposed to snack on cookie batter, but both of us nibbled on some anyhow. I heard Grandma tell Mom that she's never gotten sick on sampling cookie dough, but Mom says we need to stay on the safe side.

The aroma of the cookies baking in the oven spread throughout our entire house, and it wasn't long before John and Grace were in the kitchen begging for some. We let each of them have a couple cookies after they cooled. John rubbed his belly when he tasted our cookies, and Grace spun around in her bare feet while leaving cookie crumbs on the floor.

Dad came out next and said, "What good things are you girls doing this afternoon?" Anna Lin said, "I baked my first batch of chocolate chip cookies."

I told Dad that Anna Lin and I are baking up a storm. Dad said we could bake up a storm anytime.

I saw the Maple River Project brochure on the kitchen table. "Oh, Anna Lin, I have something important to ask you when we're done baking the cookies."

"What is it, Molly Jo?"

"Let's carry a plate of cookies upstairs to my room and discuss it there," I said.

So, Anna Lin poured us two glasses of milk, and I carried two napkins and four cookies for us, plus the brochure. This would be the first time Anna Lin sees my room, and I wondered what she will think of it.

As we climbed the stairs, Anna Lin said, "So you go up the stairs every time you want to go to your room?"

"Well, yes, Anna Lin. How else would I get there if I didn't go up the stairs?" She just smiled and said, "I don't know."

Anna Lin's eyes turned round as saucers as she gazed around my room with her mouth gaping open. I was a little wound up inside, wondering what she would think because my room is still very plain, and I share my room with my little sister.

But her eyes were wide open when she exclaimed, "I love it, Molly Jo! I wish I had an upstairs room like yours. I always wanted to have an upstairs, but my house is all downstairs."

She scampered over to the window and gazed out of it for at least five minutes. I guess she's never seen the view from an upstairs bedroom before. She waved to cars driving by and people walking their dogs.

She said, "I see a bird's nest in your big tree, Molly Jo."

At first, I thought she was being silly, but I suppose if it's your first time to have an upstairs room, it must be exciting. For my whole life, my room has been upstairs. I never even thought it was unique until now when I saw it through Anna Lin's eyes. She's made me realize that my room is perfectly fine.

I like Anna Lin because she notices little things. She's a keeper kind of friend, and I know we will get along well. I could feel it in my heart.

In a moment of awkwardness, Anna turned away from the window overlooking the front yard and said to me, "Molly Jo, did you know that I'm adopted?"

"Wow, you're adopted, Anna Lin? That must mean you're doubly special. Your parents chose you!"

"Yes, and I wouldn't want it any other way. They are the best parents."

For sure, I knew that I have the best parents too. Plus, I have Grandma. As we sat on my brand new red and yellow quilt, eating our freshly baked cookies, I showed Anna Lin the Maple River Project brochure from Mr. Simmons.

I didn't expect her to show any enthusiasm about the project, but she rested her chin on her hand, and I could see her brain was working. She had so many questions about when the project needs to be completed and can she be a part of it. Soon, my head was about to pop through the roof! Like in an incredibly exhilarating way!

I got out my journal and began writing all the ideas we came up with together. We used our imagination and curiosity to figure out what would help make new families happy.

We won't be doing all of these, but one or two of them could be perfect. Here are our ideas so far...

- Bake cookies for new families and share the recipe with them

- Ask Grandma if she would make a quilt for every new family

- Create a welcoming committee at school for new kids

- Give tickets for free ice cream cones

- Create a coloring book that tells new families about the fun things to do in Maple River

I am surprised, I must say that this project doesn't seem so bad after all. Anna Lin and I had fun coming up with these ideas.

Suddenly we heard knocking on my bedroom door. I opened the door slowly, and it was Grandma and Grace. Grandma peeked her head in and said, "Grace and I have been playing games while you girls have been working. Would it be alright for Grace to play with you two for a little while? She's just dying to do that."

My eyes locked with Anna Lin's eyes. Nothing came out of our mouths until a few seconds later, when we both started laughing uncontrollably. "Yes, Grandma, Grace is welcome to come in." After all, I was happy that Anna Lin and I got a bunch of time together, just the two of us.

Grace came in whispering in my ear as if it were a secret. "Would Anna Lin twirl in her skirt?"

Anna Lin overheard what Grace said, and she just smiled and nodded.

"Sure," she said to Grace. "Do you have a twirly skirt?"

"No, but I wished I did," Grace said.

"Maybe Grandma could sew one for you. Watch me spin around, Grace." And so, she did. She spun and twisted

and whirled around my room while her blue skirt with flyaway ribbons floated in the air – until she lost her balance and toppled onto the floor.

"Oh, I feel sick, very sick," she said.

Grace and I gave out a gasp. And even though I stood still, I also had to brace myself. Yuck, what a terrible sickish feeling! I can only imagine how Anna Lin must feel.

Grace's mouth was wide open, and her eyes full of surprise. She said, "What happened?" After all, she probably never guessed twirling could be dangerous! She patted Anna Lin and told her, "I'm so sorry."

Anna Lin just barely smiled while holding both hands on her forehead. She hardly moved at first, and her face became so pale. Slowly, she got up, first to her knees, and then shakily on her legs. But she got up. Whew.

We sat on my bed again, hoping the dizziness would get out of our heads. Anna Lin said, "Let's do something else." And we all agreed.

But then Dad knocked on the door and said, "Anna Lin, your father is here to pick you up."

All three of us gave out a big, "Aww!" We didn't want the afternoon to end. And we had barely started on the Maple River project. So, what now?

Anna Lin left, carrying her plate of cookies. I was already missing her and realizing that Anna Lin was probably the one thing that Grandma spoke about. Having a best friend is my one thing. I found my new best friend right here in Maple River, and it is Anna Lin! She makes all the difference.

This was one of those Saturdays that I'll always remember. Every little thing was coming together until something most unexpectedly happened, and I wanted to just hide forever.

CHAPTER 24:
THE BIG MISTAKE I MADE

That evening when our family sat down to dinner, Mom asked if Anna Lin and I discussed the MRP. You know, the Maple River Project. I told her I needed to dash upstairs and grab the scribbly notes in my journal. Mom smacked her lips and smiled.

I ran upstairs, and my journal was still wide open on my bed, but oh no! I left the lid off my pen, and my pen leaked! My new red and yellow quilt now has a big blue stain. Ack!

My heart nearly popped out of my chest. I felt my eyes getting teary, and I kept trying to blink them away. What on earth am I going to do? I covered the stain with my pillow and ran downstairs with my journal to the kitchen.

Forks were clanging, and everybody was passing dishes around the table. Dad said, "Please sit down, Molly Jo. Your dinner is getting cold."

Dinner had been served on my plate: a baked sweet potato with melted butter and sour cream, peas (yuck), and a chicken patty on a bun with lettuce. I love this meal except for the peas, but all I could think of was that blue ink stain on my brand-new quilt.

My face felt red-hot, and I wished more than anything else that I would have been more careful. Grandma will be so disappointed in me for being careless.

She will think I don't care about my new quilt, but that couldn't be further from the truth. Mom said, "Please share some of those creative MRP ideas with us, Molly Jo. The ones in your journal."

Dad said, "Maybe we should let the poor girl eat first. She's hungry."

I tried to force my mouth to smile, but that was impossible. I couldn't eat much, only taking a few nibbles. How will I keep that ink stain hidden from Grandma? She worked so hard sewing my brand-new quilt, and now I've totally ruined it. What kind of girl am I?

"Are you feeling alright, Molly Jo?" Mom asked. She must have known something was not right because she read my mind.

"Yes, I am okay," I said with a crackly voice.

But I wasn't okay, not at all.

Grandma said, "Molly Jo, something is clearly bothering you. And unless the sky is falling, it's probably not worth your concern, dear girl."

I blurted out without thinking and said, "But you don't understand, Grandma. You don't get it."

I did everything I could to stall the ocean of tears from swallowing up my eyes. Nobody at the table had a single idea of why I was such a wreck. Everything was fine before I went upstairs to get my journal, but now, I can't believe myself. Of all the people I didn't want to let down, that would be my Grandma.

So, I just said it. I shouted it out.

"I've ruined my red and yellow quilt, Grandma. And I don't know how to make it better. And I am as sorry as I can be, but it was just a terrible, awful mistake."

"That has made you this upset?" Grandma said.

"Yes, and I promise I won't ever bother you to make me anything again."

"Well, unless your quilt is in a million pieces or has flown away, I am sure we can repair it together. It can't be that bad, Molly Jo. Let's finish dinner, and then we can examine the quilt together," Grandma said.

Grace just stared at me and wondered why I was so crazy upset.

"Are you going to be alright, Molly Jo?" Grace asked in her innocent style.

John just kept gulping down his meal. In fact, he had a second chicken sandwich. Dad re-heated the food on my plate, and Mom suggested that I share the Maple River Project ideas in my notebook.

I took a deep breath after Grandma told me that we can fix it together no matter what it is. Suddenly, I noticed that my worry disappeared like a feather that's whisked away by the wind.

I chomped down my chicken patty and sweet potato. I wish I had more Grandma-kind-of-thinking in my head. She hopes for the best, but I expect the worst. Why do I do this over and over?

John said, "I know what you did today, Molly Jo."

"What do you mean, John?"

"I learned about making mountains out of meatloaf," John said.

Mom covered her mouth with her hand, but I knew she was laughing, and then Dad and Grandma chuckled, too.

"You mean, making a mountain out of a molehill, John?" Dad said.

"Oh yeah, Dad, that's what I meant," John said, while shaking his head and getting a little red. "Saying meatloaf was super-duper funny," he said, laughing out loud.

Dad said, "Well, Molly Jo considered the problem with her quilt to be as big as a mountain, but Grandma has assured her it's not a mountain. The problem is small, like a molehill. Molly Jo's quilt, no matter what's wrong with it, can be remedied," said Dad.

"Yes, that's right," Grandma said.

"Well, let's have Molly Jo tell us her ideas for the Maple River Project," Mom said.

Now that everyone gave their two cents, as Grandma likes to say, I opened my journal to share the ideas that Anna Lin and I came up with.

"Those are the ideas we have, Mom."

Ideas to Welcome Families to Maple River

- Bake cookies for new families and share the recipe with them

- Ask Grandma if she would make a quilt for every new family

- Create a student welcoming committee at school for new kids.

- Give tickets for free ice cream cones

- Create a coloring book that tells new families about the fun things to do in Maple River

Hmmm. These ideas sounded great when Anna Lin and I wrote them down in her perfect penmanship, but now that I've said them out loud, I wonder how good they are.

Grace said, "I love ice cream cones. Let's do that." Dad said, "Sounds like you girls have put a lot of thought into this. You and Anna Lin should figure out which two or three of your ideas would work the best.

Have you talked to Grandma about making quilts? The ice cream shop needs to be involved if you want to have coupons."

Once again, Grace said, "I like the free ice cream cones, Dad."

"Grace, Grace. Molly Jo and Anna Lin will decide which of their ideas will work best."

Grandma said, "Maybe I can sew one quilt, and then we'll hold a raffle."

I guess Anna Lin and I have many more things to figure out.

Crowd Your Mind with Good Thoughts
Advice for a Remarkable Life

If you load up your mind with good thoughts, you will crowd out everything else. This may sound too simple, but realize it takes much practice. Our brains prefer to focus on not-so-good things. If you can make it a habit to fill up your mind with good things, you will be rewarded!

Think of an empty glass jar. Imagine pouring positive thoughts into it until it's completely full. Now try pouring some yucky feelings in there. There is no room, right? That's why you must put in your best thoughts first. This is not hard, but you must repeatedly practice until you can do it without even thinking.

Why is it better to have your mind full of positive things than filled with anxious, unhappy thoughts? When your head is filled with useful, fun, and hopeful ideas, it's natural to expect more good stuff because when you search for good, you will find it. Likewise, if you look for bad, you will also find that.

Imagine this: You have a gift for someone that consists of writing paper and a pen. A person whose mind is filled with good things might think, "Awesome, I can use this paper to draw something cool or create a list of ideas. I could make paper airplanes, write a letter to someone, cut snowflakes, or make a journal. Thank you, this is great!"

The person with the not-so-good thoughts might think, "What a silly gift to receive. Why did they even bother?"

Do you see the difference? A mind filled with good things is grateful, happy, and fun. Your thoughts are a powerful force inside you. Choose your thoughts with great care because they matter more than you know.

CHAPTER 25:
A TALL GUEST AT OUR SCHOOL

The next day, at school, Ms. Jewel made a totally out-of-the-blue, but very curious announcement. She said that we would have an assembly in the afternoon, and a special guest was coming to speak to our school about having a hobby.

Hobby? I have hobbies. I am great at baking the best tasting cookies. I love to paint and make happy cards for people. I know how to draw fancy letters. I like to walk super-duper fast.

Ms. Jewel said we need to work extra hard this morning to get all our work done before the special guest arrives. Since our lunch break will be short, we will have our sack lunches in our classroom today. Wow, this must be some guest!

She passed out small pieces of paper to each of us and told us to print our names on them and then jot down one hobby that we have or that we wished we would have. I wrote "baking cookies" on mine. I wanted to list ALL my hobbies. Then she told us to fold our paper in half and drop it in the cardboard box on her desk. After I did, I wished I would have written calligraphy instead, but it was too late.

At 1:30, something caught my eye outside our classroom window, and I did a double take. I probably did a triple take. I couldn't believe what my eyes were explaining to me.

A very tall wooden giraffe rolled down the sidewalk in the front of our school. I blinked, and then I blinked again. I rubbed my eyes to see if what I was seeing, I was really seeing. This giraffe resembled the giraffe at Mr. and Mrs. Simmons' house. It looked precisely like Rudy! My eyes just about exploded out of my head and dropped to the floor.

Rudy rolled into our school on a silver metal cart that Mr. and Mrs. Simmons were pushing. I know for 100% sure that it is Mr. Simmons because of the yellow plaid pants he is wearing. I wanted to shout something like, "I know who that is," but no words would come out of my mouth. I was speechless! Being one of the newest kids at my school, I might be the only kid who knows about Rudy. Well, me and John.

Why in the world would Rudy be coming to our school? Is he our special guest?

Other kids in my class started noticing Rudy out the window too. They were pointing and getting out of their chairs to see him. Anna Lin began to spin around in her twirly skirt. Ms. Jewel loudly clapped her hands three times and said, "Everyone, please stay in your seats. You will soon learn why a giraffe is coming to our school. Stay calm, so that our surprise is the absolute best it can be."

I raised my hand high in the air and waved at Ms. Jewel with all my might. She wondered why and came over to my desk.

"I know all about that giraffe, Ms. Jewel!" I said.

"Oh, wonderful, Molly Jo. Please keep it quiet from the rest of the class. If you already know, then you are one lucky girl."

Ms. Jewel told us we needed to remain in our seats and to be very silent. The big surprise will be shared with us soon.

At 2 pm, we lined up to head over to the gymnasium, where we have special meetings at school. As we took our places in the bleachers, the kids in my class exchanged ideas about the giraffe. I heard one boy in my class say, "Somebody will WIN that giraffe and take him home!"

Oh no, that absolutely cannot, and must not be correct. The Simmons would never ever let their Rudy be donated as a prize.

Or would they? I know I am not doing a particularly good job of filling my head with good thoughts.

After everyone took a seat in the gymnasium, our principal, Mr. Dasher, challenged us to become silent. Soon the only sounds we heard were a few muffled coughs and sniffles.

Mr. Dasher proudly introduced our special guests.

He said, "Boys and girls, we are truly honored and delighted to welcome Mr. and Mrs. Chuck Simmons, the owners of Simmons Hobby Shop, to our school today. And along with them is a surprise guest!"

Does Mr. Dasher even know that Mr. and Mrs. Simmons are my *across-the-street* neighbors?

Mr. and Mrs. Simmons paraded onto the stage with Rudy on the pushcart. The kids were gasping and clapping when they saw Rudy.

I just cannot believe that Rudy, my neighbor's giraffe, is at my school! I felt like my buttons were about to pop off and bounce across the room. If only Grandma knew what was happening right here right now!

In his great loud voice, Mr. Simmons said, "Thank you, thank you, children of Maple River Elementary. Mrs. Simmons and I are as excited as two baby birds to be here." Everyone laughed and cheered.

Then Mr. Simmons pointed to Rudy and said, "Children, this – this giraffe – means the world to Mrs. Simmons and me. Not just because he is seven feet tall nor that his adorable name is Rudy. And it's not because he's a giraffe, although both the Mrs. and I love giraffes. We really do!

"But the reason that Rudy means so much to us is that someone near and dear to us made him. How many of you remember Christopher Silver, who used to attend Maple River Elementary?"

The fifth graders cheered and started chanting, "Christopher, Christopher, Christopher."

Mr. Simmons said, "Sounds like you remember Christopher well. Even though his family relocated last spring to Cape Elizabeth, he and his Dad found time in their busy schedules to be here with us today. Please put your hands together for Christopher and his Dad, Mr. Silver."

Everyone stood up and cheered as Christopher strolled onto the stage with his Dad. His Dad wore a blue denim apron kind of like my Dad and Uncle Jim wear in their woodshop. And Christopher toted two gift bags.

Mr. Simmons said, "So let me tell you a few words about Christopher and his Dad. They were our neighbors for many years right across the street from us. One thing I always admired about them is the love they have for their hobbies!

"So, Mr. Silver and Christopher, welcome back to Maple River! Will you tell the children about your hobbies?"

Mr. Silver said, "Thank you for such a big welcome. Christopher and I are thrilled to be back in Maple River for the day. We might even visit the ice cream shop while we are here. But let us tell you about our hobbies.

"I have always loved tinkering with wood and glue and nails and such. When I was a kid, I built a treehouse with my Dad, and that's when I got hooked on making things."

"Christopher, how about if you would tell us about your hobbies now?"

"Well, I-I-I like carving wood. My Dad taught me how to do this, and now I love making things too."

Mr. Simmons said, "Tell us about some things you have carved, Christopher."

"I've made some wooden spoons for my Mom, and I made each of my brothers an owl and a turtle," Christopher said.

"And, and, and?" said Mr. Simmons.

"Oh yes, and I made Rudy, this big giraffe, with the help of my Dad."

Mrs. Simmons placed her hands over her heart. She spoke into the microphone, saying, "Rudy is one of the most meaningful gifts anyone has ever given us, Christopher. He's a big friend in our house, and everyone that comes to meet him absolutely loves him. And every time I see him, I think of you and your family and how much love you put into him."

"Thank you, Mrs. Simmons," said Christopher.

Mr. Silver said, "Children, one Saturday morning last summer, while we were neighbors of Mr. and Mrs. Simmons, we saw them tearing down their old cedar fence. Christopher and I looked at each other and thought the same thing at the same time: What could we make with those old cedar fence slats that they will toss away? We are always searching for a new project.

"We asked Mr. Simmons if we could have some of those fence slats, and he said we could grab as many as we wanted. So, Christopher and I loaded up our wheelbarrow and took load after load across the street to our house."

Then Mr. Simmons said, "But I never questioned Christopher and his Dad about their plans with the fence slats. I wanted to be amazed by their woodworking wizardry!"

Mr. Silver said, "Christopher, the great kid he is, recalled how much the Simmons love safari animals. He wondered if we could build them a life-sized giraffe.

"I told him we probably couldn't make it life-size because that would be 15 or more feet tall. But we could make him tall. So, for a few weeks, I did what I like to do; I cut the fence slats into puzzle pieces and assembled them in the shape of a giraffe. Then Christopher did what he likes to do. He carved Rudy's spots and eyes. We both finished him by sanding and staining him.

210

"And, children, the mane. Can you see Rudy's mane? It's from yarn that Christopher's Mom let us use. Christopher made the mane by wrapping yarn around a long stick until it was enough to go along the back of Rudy's neck."

I couldn't believe my eyes and ears. This must be the Christopher who used to live in my house. How much crazier can this day get? Grandma, Mom, and Dad will never believe all of this. And nobody but me knows about Christopher leaving that secret book at our house.

My whole body was in total shock.

Mr. Simmons said, "Now, children, one of the best ways to have a happy life is to have a hobby, something you enjoy doing, something you love to think about. Now please, listen up. How many of you have a hobby?" said Mr. Simmons.

Kids started waving their hands in the air with all their might.

"What are some hobbies you have, children?"

Matthew said he likes to gaze at stars through a telescope with his Dad. Nick said that he likes bird watching – like Grandma! And Sarah said she likes to do scrapbooking.

Mr. Simmons said, "This is wonderful, children. You probably do not understand how amazing a hobby can be in your life. And some of you will have many hobbies in your lifetime. Mrs. Simmons loves to do calligraphy, which is fancy handwriting. It makes her so happy to even think about it."

Then Mr. Dasher made an announcement.

"Boys and girls, do you like Rudy?"

Everybody started clapping and cheering and whistling. I almost thought I'd have to put my fingers in my ears – it was that loud!

Mr. Dasher said, "Christopher and his Dad have something quite special for us today."

Oh, no, no, no, no! This cannot be coming true. Rudy cannot be given away! I thought my heart would stop, and I covered my mouth in total shock. Rudy belongs to the Simmons family and nobody else. He's a part of their family. End. Period.

Mr. Dasher continued by saying, "Two lucky children will take home a miniature Rudy today. Christopher and his Dad made two small Rudy's, just like the giant Rudy.

Miniature Rudy? Oh, my racing heart!

"Each of you should have written your name and your hobby on a piece of paper. We have your papers here in this giant bin, and Christopher will help me shake them all up and draw two names of lucky children."

Everybody held their breath and clenched their hands together while Christopher reached into the bin and chose the first name and then the second name.

Mr. Dasher said, "Drum roll, please." And everybody started stomping their feet on the bleachers. The excitement was through the roof!

"The first student to win a miniature Rudy is --- Benjamin from Ms. Samantha's 4th-grade class. And the second student to take home a miniature Rudy is --- is Everett from Mr. Stevens 5th-grade class. Please come to the stage to get your prizes!"

Christopher gave both Benjamin and Everett one of the gift bags he brought onto the stage. I am so glad that they were not giving away the real Rudy. That would have made my heart crumble into a million tiny pieces all over the floor.

Mr. Simmons told us that the real Rudy would stay in the front lobby of our school for the next two days so that every student would have time to see him up-close.

Mr. Dasher stepped onto the stage again and announced, "Boys and girls, let's give our guests a big hand. We all thank Mr. and Mrs. Chuck Simmons, Rudy the giraffe, Christopher Silver, and his father, Mr. Silver. What an honor to have each of you today."

Everyone cheered loudly, and Mr. Dasher spoke into the microphone and said, "Now, quiet, please. Let me say one more thing. Remember what you learned today about how much joy a hobby can bring you. All my life, I have loved fishing. Even the thought of going fishing brings me happiness, and that is what I wish for each of you here, a hobby that rewards your heart with happiness. You may now go quietly back to your classrooms."

I couldn't have made up a story this good about Rudy visiting our school. I can't wait to tell the kids in my class that Rudy is my across-the-street neighbor! They won't believe it! Well, I hope they do because it's true. It's popping-my-buttons amazing that I'm the only kid who already knows Rudy.

Do Your Hardest Work First
Advice for a Remarkable Life

When you have a list of things to accomplish in your day, choose the hardest thing first and get it done right away.

That way, the rest of your day will be more comfortable and fun. Most people will put off their hardest thing and do the easy stuff first. But the hardest thing is still there, waiting for you to tackle it. So just do it first, when your mind is fresh, and your body is wide awake.

Then you can thank yourself and feel good about what you have accomplished.

Let's say you had these three things to get done today:
- Clean your room
- Do your Social Studies homework
- Rake leaves in the yard

Which of these is hardest for you? Why not get it done first? Wouldn't that feel great? Then you can tackle another thing on your list. Work on that hard task until it's finished. You may need to take breaks to refresh your mind or body along the way but keep going.

If you get nothing else done, except the hardest thing, you can take great pleasure that it's done. The rest will be more pleasant to tackle.

Yes, there are exceptions. Sometimes you may have an easy task that is important to get done first, like turning in your homework. Use your good judgment, but when you can, tackle the hard jobs first, and you will be glad you did.

CHAPTER 26:
THE SILVER LINING

The weekend arrived! Dad asked John to go to work with him on Saturday morning, and I held back my tears because Grace and I weren't allowed to go.

Grandma said, "Let Dad and John have their guy time! You and Grace will have your turns to go to work with Dad some other time. Besides, there might be a silver lining."

Silver lining? I've heard Grandma say this once before, but I'm not sure what that means.

Mom said, "A silver lining is like a nice gift, a sort of surprise when things are gloomy."

Mom said she made peanut brittle one time, but it didn't get hard and crunchy like it was supposed to do. She didn't want to waste all those peanuts, so she melted the peanut brittle with boiling water until the only thing remaining was the peanuts.

Then she roasted the peanuts in the oven, and she made the peanut brittle all over again – but this time from the roasted peanuts. She said this time, it was the best peanut brittle in the world. Even though it was kind of a disaster the first time around, it was the best peanut brittle the next time.

So, Grace and I wondered what the silver lining could be for us. Grandma said, "First, you must believe in silver linings. Now go about your morning and have fun."

The telephone rang, and I could hear Mom saying, "Uh-huh, uh-huh. Sure! That would be wonderful. About what time can she be here?"

Who is coming to our house? Who could it be?

Mom said, "I'll tell the girls, so they are ready."

Then she hung up the phone.

"Girls, Anna Lin is coming over to play. She has something for Grace, and she can stay to have lunch with us."

Could this be the silver lining that Grandma was talking about?

Anna Lin's Dad drove her over, and she brought her backpack. Mom answered the door and Anna Lin bolted in with a smile a mile wide. I'm so lucky to have a happy friend like her.

Grace wrinkled her forehead. She couldn't believe that Anna Lin wasn't wearing one of her swirly skirts.

Anna Lin said, "Grace, I brought you something that you are going to love."

"What is it?" said Grace.

Anna Lin unzipped her backpack and pulled out three of her skirts. She said, "These don't fit me anymore, Grace. Now they are yours!"

Grace's face was as radiant as the sunshine after the rain. She tried all the skirts on, right over her clothes - not just one of them, all of them at the same time. Mom didn't mind. None of us cared. It was a major moment for Grace as she twirled around the room, making herself dizzy.

Mom warmed some tomato soup and my favorite grilled cheese sandwiches for lunch. Anna Lin and I set the table with spoons and paper napkins, and soon we heard Dad's truck pull into the driveway.

"John and Dad are back," said Mom. "And just in time for lunch."

We waited and waited, but they didn't come right into the house. Mom said for us girls to eat our soup while it's hot; she and Grandma would investigate.

Soon we heard Dad say, "Could somebody please open the door? We need a little help here."

So, Grandma opened the squeaky screen door, and the guys came in carrying something big. Something they made from wood. I wasn't sure at first what it was, but then I realized it's a window bench for our bedroom. Could it be? Could it be?

Dad said, "We tried our best, girls, to make a perfect seat for you two to lounge on and watch out your window. Hopefully, it's what you two imagined!"

I couldn't believe it. I just couldn't believe it. It's better than we imagined.

So, this was why Grace and I didn't go with Dad and John this morning. This is a marvel of marvels! I am so glad that Anna Lin is here to witness this. It's more than a silver lining; it might even be a gold lining!

We all headed up to my bedroom. The bench was heavy, so Mom helped Dad and John get it up the stairs. They placed it under the window, and it fit perfectly! Dad said there would be a few adjustments he and John would need to make. And then he showed Grace and I the secret compartment beneath the bench seat where we could store things.

217

Grandma said, "I will make a red and yellow cushion for your bench and a pillow for each corner."

It was the best Saturday morning ever.

John said, "Molly Jo, you won't believe what I got to do while we were at the woodshop."

"What, John?"

"I got to fly the drone! I got to navigate it by myself. Well, Uncle Jim helped me, but I got to do it. It was not easy, but Uncle Jim said I have to get muscle memory, and it will be easier."

I asked, "What's muscle memory, John?"

"It's kind of like when you tie your shoes. Your fingers know what to do without thinking about every single step."

"Oh, I get it! I can even talk to somebody while tying my shoes, and my fingers know what to do."

"Yeah, that's muscle memory. Uncle Jim said I did well for my first time. Next time we go there, I can show you how to fly the drone, Molly Jo."

I was happy for John. It was the one thing he for sure wanted to do in Maine. And he got to do it.

Anna Lin asked if she could lounge on our new window bench, and both Grace and I said, "Yes, we have room for all three of us!"

I love that Anna Lin thinks our house is the best because she is right!

Mom said, "How about you girls finish up the Maple River Project today? I will call Anna Lin's Mom and ask if she can stay till dinner."

We ran back downstairs to finish eating our lukewarm tomato soup and grilled cheese sandwiches. We didn't really give a hoot because we're heading right back upstairs to sit on our new window bench.

I asked Mom if she would make us girls fluffernutter sandwiches for a treat this afternoon, and I could hardly believe this, but she said yes.

I thought my ears would run around the block; they were so happy. I never in my life would guess she'd say yes to super sweet fluffernutter sandwiches.

She said, "You are only kids once, and one fluffernutter sandwich won't kill you. Besides, we're Mainers now and when in Maine, do what the Mainers do. But only once in a blue moon, Molly Jo. The sugar in this is off-the-charts."

At that moment, I didn't care if this would be the only time we'd get to eat fluffernutter sandwiches. At least we will today! And as Mr. Simmons would say, it was super-duper delicious.

Anna Lin and I spent the rest of the afternoon putting our heads together. We came up with our best idea for the Maple River Project. We want to create a Welcome to Maple River coloring book for new people in our town.

Anna Lin will oversee drawing the pictures, and she will enlist a few other kids to help. I will do the fancy lettering on each page. We will have coupons for free ice cream cones too.

And once a year, Anna Lin and I will bake cookies and have a welcome party at the Simmons Hobby for all the new people who move to Maple River. All we must do is get our plan approved by the committee. I hope Mr. and Mrs. Simmons like our ideas!

Anna Lin and I wrote our ideas in perfect lettering on a big poster board. Grandma wants us to do the most good for new people in our town. Anna Lin and I hope we are doing the most good.

After Anna Lin left, Grace and I relaxed on our new window seat. We made a big thank you sign for Dad and John for making the bench for us.

Have a Hobby
Advice for a Remarkable Life

Oh, the joy a hobby can give you. Do you have a hobby? Not everyone does, but if you do, you know how much fun, hope, and peace a hobby can add to your life.

What are some hobbies? The list of hobbies is endless but here are several to inspire you: watching birds, drawing, playing board games, collecting leaves or rocks, reading books, listening to music, putting together puzzles, collecting postage stamps, baking, playing an instrument, woodworking, learning how to juggle, gardening, sewing, and learning a different language.

Why is it useful to have a hobby? A hobby will save you from dull, dreary days. A hobby will give you something to think about, hope for, and use your imagination. A hobby can connect you to other people who have similar interests. Or if you prefer quiet times, there are plenty of hobbies for that as well.

You need not spend a lot of money on a hobby. Sometimes what you choose to do is absolutely free, or you may need minimal supplies. If you enjoy your hobby with a friend, you can share supplies.

Even when you don't have time to spend on your hobby, you can still have fun thinking about it, imagining what you might do next, or planning your next project. A hobby you enjoy will fill your heart with delight.

Hobbies expand your world, make you smarter, more creative, and engaging. A hobby will make your life more interesting and fun. Hobbies are gold!

CHAPTER 27:
WILL OUR IDEAS FLY?

M om told me that Mr. and Mrs. Simmons are coming over for dessert and hearing our MRP ideas this weekend. I started second-guessing whether the plan Anna Lin and I brainstormed was good enough.

Mom said, "Molly Jo, you and Anna Lin can present your MRP ideas to Mr. Simmons. He will introduce them to the committee next week. So just be confident and speak your thoughts with certainty and clarity.

"If he believes that you and Anna Lin have confidence in your ideas, he will want to share them with the committee. If he feels that you are wishy-washy, then I'm not sure what he'll want to do."

I said, "I am *pretty sure* we are confident, but let me ask Anna Lin to be sure."

"Alright, honey. Confidence is particularly important. If you want to run your ideas past Dad and me first, you can do that. Grandma would love hearing them too. That way, you can rehearse."

I said, "Maybe Anna Lin can come home with me tomorrow after school and spend the night."

Mom said, "That will work. I will ask her parents."

Anna Lin's parents agreed and said that she could ride the bus home with me tomorrow after school.

The next day Anna Lin and I studied our plan in my room. We read it over and over and wondered what questions the grown-ups will ask us.

Anna Lin said, "Maybe this is a good time for us to share our ideas with your family. That way, they can help us improve our ideas before we share them with Mr. Simmons."

"Great idea," I said. "Let me round everyone up!"

Mom and Dad were cleaning up the kitchen, and Grandma was playing cards with Grace. John and William were in Cherry Forest searching for gold.

I managed to round them all up around the kitchen table. Dad said, "Okay, girls, tell us what you've got!"

Anna Lin and I just looked at each other and started giggling.

"You go," I said to Anna Lin.

"No, you go!" she said back to me.

Dad said, "Are you both presenting or just one of you?"

Oops, we hadn't figured that part out yet. So, we whispered back and forth to each other. Anna Lin agreed she would talk about the coloring book, and I would talk about the poster and the cookies.

Anna Lin cleared her throat and took in a giant gulp of air. She said, "Molly Jo and I will create a Maple River Coloring Book that will be given to the new people in our town. The pictures in the book will be places from our downtown area and around. Places that families will love!

"I will draw some of the pictures, and we will get other kids to help with the rest. Molly Jo will print captions for all the pictures in her fancy letters. We will both make a colorful cover!"

Then I took my turn. I said, "Anna Lin and I are also going to create a poster for our school with a list of ways to welcome new kids. We brought it up with Ms. Jewel, and she will get our class to help. In fact, she said maybe we could have a whole welcoming committee for new kids.

"And once a year, Anna Lin and I will bake cookies for a big cookie party at the Simmons Hobby Shop and invite everyone new. This is our plan! Do you like it?"

Grandma said, "Wow, that's a plan, girls! I hope you will include a picture of Rudy in your coloring book. He is someone who will make many people happy."

Mom said, "How about a cookie party two times a year instead of one? Spring and fall? And maybe there can be a coupon for Simmons Hobby Shop in the coloring book since the party will be there if they agree."

John said, "Can Mr. Kim be in the coloring book? He's not part of the downtown scene, but he's the best bus driver we ever had!"

Dad said, "You girls have invested some hard work in this project. More details need to be ironed out, but your preliminary plan sounds ready for Mr. Simmons."

Grandma clenched her hands and said, "Your hearts are in the right place, girls. Let's see what happens!"

I couldn't stop dwelling on what Mom said: "If Mr. Simmons believes that Anna Lin and I have confidence in our plans, he will want to share them with the committee."

Now that we've rehearsed, Anna Lin and I understand our ideas forward and backward. We're a team, a powerful team, at least I think we are. Anna Lin and I have never done a project this big. We don't know if it will get approved, but we are crossing our hearts and fingers.

CHAPTER 28:
FINDING HOME AGAIN

The weekend came, and I was up in my room relaxing on our window bench when Grace asked, "Can we read that magic book, Molly Jo?"

"Magic book, Grace?"

"You know, the one we found in our closet shelf, Molly Jo. You said it didn't have pictures in it, but I don't care. I still want to read it with you."

Okay, Grace, if you really want to read it with me, then let's do it. So, Grace sat on the window bench with me, she in one corner and me in the other. I opened to the place where I left off – "Do Your Hardest Work First."

Grace thought for a moment and said, "Does that mean I should clean my room first, Molly Jo? That's hard for me!"

I said, "Yes, Grace, that's the idea because cleaning your room is hard for you. But for me, that's easy because I love cleaning our room. So, for me, I would choose to do my Social Studies work because that's not fun for me. It's different for everyone."

"Molly Jo, whoever wrote this book is smart. I want to do the hardest work first."

"Grace, it was Mr. Simmons! Mr. Simmons wrote this book."

"Mr. Simmons, our neighbor?"

"Yes, and he doesn't know we already have his book. Remember that day at the Hobby Shop, and you saw more of these exact books for sale? That's when Mr. Simmons said he was the one who wrote the book."

"Is it okay that we have it, Molly Jo?"

"I think so. Someone named Christopher left it here, and I wonder if he's the boy who used to live here. He came to our school one day."

"Are you going to return it to him, Molly Jo?"

"I probably should, Grace. I would like to keep it, but you're right. We should tell Mom and Dad about it."

We both went downstairs with our book and showed Dad. Dad put on his reading glasses, glanced at it for what seemed a long time, and said kind of seriously, "For how long have you two had this book?"

"Since we moved in, Dad," I said while trying to keep my voice from trembling. "We thought it was secretly left for Grace and me."

"Even though in the front it says it's for Christopher from Mr. Simmons?"

"But Dad, we didn't know who they were back then."

"Well, girls, it's always best to do the right thing. And even though you didn't do the right thing right away, you are doing it now."

Dad said, "The good news, girls, is that this is a wonderful book. Your Mom and I just heard about it from an article we read in the paper. Mr. Simmons is getting an award for authoring this little book. Imagine that!"

Dad waded through a pile of papers on the table until he found the article he clipped. He picked it up and read:

"Longtime Maple River resident, Mr. Charles Simmons, will be presented the Maple River Children's Author of the

Year for his book, "Advice for a Remarkable Life." Mr. Simmons told the Maple River Gazette that he has had this book in his head since he was a kid and raised by his grandparents. They taught him these life lessons in the tiny cabin where they lived.

"Mr. Simmons visits schools, churches, and parents' groups hoping to spread these lessons that shaped his life and legacy. His book can be purchased at Simmons Hobby Shop or online. Every year, he donates hundreds of his books to local libraries and schools."

Grace said, "Mr. Simmons is real, real smart, Dad!"

"Yes, we are fortunate to be his neighbors. I can't imagine a finer neighborhood than right here, across the street from the Simmons.

"And the other thing we read in the article is about the last page of the book. Did you notice the last page?"

"Last page, Dad?" I said. "We haven't read that far."

"Well, let's take a look."

I opened the book to the last page, and there was something tiny that said, "PIFWYD."

"PIFWYD. What does that mean, Dad?"

"The first part means 'Pay It Forward.' That's why Christopher probably left the book in your closet. He wants you to have the book now. And WYD means "When You're Done." When you're done reading it, you can pay it forward to someone else."

"Maybe we can pay it forward to Anna Lin or Melissa," Grace said.

"Or to John," Dad said.

I didn't really want to give away this book. It has important things for me to learn, and I want to have a remarkable life. But maybe I can save my money to buy a brand-new book to share.

Dad said, "Molly Jo, maybe since Mr. Simmons lives right across the street, you can ask him about the book you found and what to do."

"But, Dad, I cannot do that. He will wonder why I didn't tell him I have his book before now."

"Molly Jo, you're making it a big deal. Just tell Mr. Simmons that you believe Christopher paid the book forward to you, and now you want to repay the favor by paying it forward to someone else. I'm sure he will have a good idea for you."

"Okay, Dad, if you think I should," I said.

The Simmons are coming over for dinner tomorrow night, and I better speak to Mr. Simmons before that! I squished my head with both of my hands, hoping something brilliant would pop in there to get me out of this mangled mess. Well, it's not really a mess, but I wish it weren't anything at all!

I told Grace that we have a plan. It was a nerve-wrecking plan, but it was a plan. We will go over to Mr. Simmons and show him that we have the book. Dad said that my plan was good.

Grace and I walked to the Simmons house and rang the doorbell. Their happy yellow front door still looked like it had just been painted, and they had two yellow polka-dot umbrellas resting on the corner of their porch. In one hand, I held the book, and in the other, I clenched Grace's hand.

We could feel the vibrations of Mr. Simmons rushing to the door, and Buffalo started to bark. The door opened wide, and there was Mr. Plaid Pants filling up the whole space. Uh, I mean Mr. Simmons. He had a giant smile. Stephen came running to the door, which put a light feeling in the air.

In his giant deep voice, Mr. Simmons said, "Why look who's here? Molly Jo and Grace Daisy. To what do we owe this visit?"

"Uh, uh, uh."

"Please come in. Mrs. Simmons will be delighted to say hello to you, too."

So, we stepped in, and I never let go of Grace's hand. Mrs. Simmons bustled over to the door with a pen in one hand and wanting to hug Grace and me with the other.

"Won't you come in and stay awhile, girls? I was just doing some fancy calligraphy for the Hobby Shop. Molly Jo, maybe you'd like to join me, and Stephen would love it if you stayed and played, Grace!"

Play? This is serious stuff. Doesn't she know we're here for something extremely important that I wish we didn't have to do? And there was Rudy, as tall and cute as ever.

"No, thank you very much, but we can't play, Mrs. Simmons. But we wanted to return this book."

Mr. Simmons said, "Oh, you purchased one of my books! Don't you like the book, girls?"

"Ooh, yes, we love it, Mr. Simmons. But it's not ours. We found it on our closet shelf, and it says it belongs to Christopher somebody. Maybe he's the boy who came to our school."

"Well, yes, that's him! He's a fine boy. And yes, I gave him my book – and he Paid It Forward, just as I hoped he would. Now I love that boy even more! And I am so glad you and Grace are now the proud owners."

"So, Grace and I want to Pay It Forward, Mr. Simmons."

"That's so admirable! Did you get to read it, Molly Jo? You know, there's great advice in that book I wrote that will help you have the best life possible – if you put my words into action."

"We haven't yet finished it, Mr. Simmons."

"Well, then keep it and read it to your heart's content. By all means, finish it. Use the advice, Molly Jo. I bet you already do. Take it from me, it works!

"And make sure that Grace and John get to read it too. Few people know this, but these are lessons I learned from my grandparents. If only I could be a fraction of the people they were! Pay your book forward when you're done so someone else may benefit from it."

I asked, "Could I use my money to buy another book to give to someone new in Maple River?"

Mr. Simmons chuckled loudly and said, "That's a grand idea, Molly Jo. No wonder you're a loyal member of the MRP. We chose you for a good reason, and the Mrs. and I cannot wait to hear your other ideas tomorrow evening."

Stephen gave Grace a metal toy car to play with, and I secretly let out the biggest sigh of relief for the way everything worked out. I knew it would. I just knew it would.

"Thank you, Mr. Simmons. Thank you, Mrs. Simmons. We will see you tomorrow."

Grace wanted to stay and play cars with Stephen. I wanted to admire Rudy and hang out at their house, but we were there on serious business, so I decided we better go back home. Besides, Dad will wonder what we are doing.

Mrs. Simmons said, "Aww, you girls have to go home so soon? You are welcome any time to come visit Stephen and Rudy."

"Thank you, Mrs. Simmons. We'll come back and play another time," I sadly said. But then I thought to ask, "Could I bring my friend Anna Lin over to meet Rudy the next time she comes to our house to play?"

"Why, of course, you can, Molly Jo. Rudy loves all the attention he gets."

As Grace and I ran back home, I heard John and William playing in Cherry Forest, with absolutely no idea about the secret book we have.

Dad was sitting on the porch swing with Grandma and looking puzzled why we were coming back home with the book. I could hear Mom playing the piano through the screen door.

I wondered if Dad and Mom know all the lessons in this book. And Grandma? For sure, Grandma does. Does knowing these things give you a remarkable life if you do what it says? I am sure it does.

I am new in Maple River, but I am not the same girl who cried a puddle of tears when we left Chesterfield Lane. I am a girl who isn't afraid to figure things out. Even when the light switches are in a different place.

I can help other kids understand that being the new kid only lasts for a short time. And sometimes it makes your life even better, like when you live across the street from a friendly giraffe named Rudy, or you find another best friend as I did.

Moving to a new place is not the end of the world as I thought way back then. In fact, it is an adventure, like Grandma says. I finally feel at home once again.

Occasionally there are rough patches, but if you look beyond them, everything works out one way or another. I have *high hopes* from this day forward.

The End.

AFTERWORD

Mr. and Mr. Simmons were pleased with Molly Jo and Anna Lin's presentation for the Maple River Project. They especially liked two ideas: the coloring book and the welcoming committee.

Molly Jo and Anna Lin spent a few weeks crafting the artwork for their coloring book. The coloring books will be fun and helpful for newcomers to learn about the attractions in and around Maple River. A coupon for free ice cream cones is included, which makes Grace super happy.

And the best part is that Maple River Elementary School will now have a Welcoming Committee headed up by Ms. Jewel. Student ambassadors will assist brand-new students in becoming familiar with their school and classmates. New kids will enjoy a greater level of feeling welcome.

Dad and Uncle Jim are making plans for a treehouse in the backyard maple tree. The details need to be figured out, but it's cautiously promising that the Daisy family will have a new treehouse in the summer, making Grandma and Mom both happy and worried.

Melissa may get to visit the Daisy family in the summer if her parents can swing it. Her Dad got an infection in his toe that spread to his leg, and he's been in the hospital a few times.

No snowy owl showed up in Cherry Forest in their first winter, but the Daisy family hopes one will. Cherry Forest holds some unexpected surprises for the Daisy family.

MEET THE AUTHOR

Thank you for reading, "Molly Jo Daisy: Being the New Kid."

I am a proud grandma and married to my best friend and high school sweetheart, Dave. I enjoy watercolor painting, making greeting cards, long walks, playing the piano, and spending time with my family.

I love writing Molly Jo Daisy stories for you, and I hope they fill you up with hope and smiles. Molly Jo and her family have become embedded in my heart.

Just about everyone faces challenges in their lives, but don't let your circumstances keep you from reaching higher. Instead, choose to shine more brightly than ever before and never give up.

Each night as you put your head on your pillow and each morning as you wake up, be grateful for your life, even the tiniest things. If you learn that one habit, you will be blessed beyond belief because you will have unlocked the power of gratefulness.

Visit us at www.facebook.com/MollyJoDaisy

Sending you a million blessings for your best life.

Mary Louise Morris

MEET MY GUEST ILLUSTRATORS

I'm quite proud of these delightful young people who submitted their artwork for this book. I am grateful for their artistry and being huge fans of Molly Jo Daisy.

Ashlyn Lindow lives in Woodville, Ohio. She is the daughter of Eric and Sherry Lindow, and granddaughter of my dear childhood friend, Virginia (Rudolph) Baumer. Ashlyn submitted these drawings: the downtown scene, the ice cream cone, and Eliza's Coffee Café. Ashlyn enjoys musicals, volleyball, basketball, reading biographies, and playing with her beagle. Thank you, Ashlyn!

Henry Morris, my grandson, lives in Herndon, Virginia. Henry encouraged me to write a chapter book as part of the Molly Jo Daisy series. He loves to swim, play soccer, do his ninja course in the backyard, and play the piano and violin. Henry drew the Maple River Fire Department illustration. Thank you, Henry!

Millie Morris, my granddaughter, lives in Mount Juliet, Tennessee. Millie is especially fond of Molly Jo's prayer book, *Molly Jo Daisy: Prayers from My Heart*. Millie is an adventuresome girl who loves school, singing, and swimming, but her most favorite activity is crafting. Millie drew the Maple River Sweet Shop illustration. Thank you, Millie Girl!

OTHER CHILDRENS BOOKS BY MARY LOUISE MORRIS

Molly Jo Daisy Not Giving Up

Nine-year-old Molly Jo Daisy learns from her teacher that kids can do more than just homework and play. Her teacher instructs the class to start working on their dreams, but Molly Jo doesn't know where to begin or what to do. What she finally figures out is quite amazing for a girl her age! Written in verse for children 5 -10.

Molly Jo Daisy We Have to Move

When Molly Jo's parents announce the family is going to move, Molly Jo's heart goes into a tailspin. She dislikes packing and sorting through everything. She truly doesn't like it when strangers walk through her home for showings. And worst of all, she doesn't not want to leave her best friend. Written in verse for children 5 -10.

Molly Jo Daisy Prayers from My Heart

In this non-traditional and humorous prayer book, Molly Jo Daisy shares her personal, heartfelt prayers with you. She wears her heart on her sleeve and speaks her heart-warming worries and concerns as only a child can. For children 5 -10.

See You in My Dreams

Have your child take a journey to enchanting, imaginary places before they drift off to sleep. Who doesn't love to think of wearing a jetpack and flying straight towards the silvery moon? A wonderful read aloud bedtime story for children 3 – 8.

Made in the USA
Las Vegas, NV
21 November 2022

59978495R00133